"Are you up for a little adventure?"

Reece remembered how excited Abby had been, and it had been just as hot for him, too. Did she still want that?

"It's been building between us ever since we were kids, Abby. It's time we took a chance on us."

Needing her answer right then, he pulled her up close to him, his hands traveling up her back and into her hair.

It was like silk. He wanted to feel it trailing over his shoulders, his chest, everywhere.

The thought made his kiss less introductory, less tentative, than it might have been otherwise. He took her soft lips and opened her mouth, swallowing a deep moan that came from her immediately. She felt so right, but better, the flames leaping between them were incredibly hot.

Her arms went around his neck, and she twined her tongue with his, as she strained to meet his every move.

He'd take that as a yes.

Dear Reader,

Christmas can be one of the most romantic times of the year, but the holidays can also bring enormous stress. What better way to escape it all than with a hot romance? That's what my heroine, Abby, is thinking, when she decides to give herself a little much-needed Christmas cheer by having a holiday fling with the boy next door, Reece Winston.

Reece is happy to oblige, as he's never quite forgotten the pretty friend he always teased in school, but now Abby is all grown up, and Reece wants to make up for lost time. Neither one of them anticipates falling in love, but Christmas is a time for surprises, too.

Best of the season to you and your family, whichever holiday you celebrate. I hope you enjoy *I'll Be Yours for Christmas* (maybe with a nice glass of wine or hot chocolate), and that Abby and Reece's story can offer you a little escape from the hustle and bustle, as well.

Happy holidays,

Samantha Hunter

Samantha Hunter

I'LL BE YOURS FOR CHRISTMAS

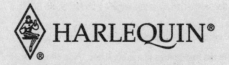

TORONTO • NEW YORK • LONDON
AMSTERDAM • PARIS • SYDNEY • HAMBURG
STOCKHOLM • ATHENS • TOKYO • MILAN • MADRID
PRAGUE • WARSAW • BUDAPEST • AUCKLAND

Recycling programs
for this product may
not exist in your area.

ISBN-13: 978-0-373-79588-8

I'LL BE YOURS FOR CHRISTMAS

ABOUT THE AUTHOR

Samantha Hunter lives in Syracuse, New York, where she writes full-time for Harlequin Books. When she's not plotting her next story, Sam likes to work in her garden, quilt, cook, read and spend time with her husband and their dogs. Most days you can find Sam chatting on the Harlequin Blaze boards at eHarlequin.com, or you can check out what's new, enter contests or drop her a note at her website, www.samanthahunter.com.

Books by Samantha Hunter

HARLEQUIN BLAZE
142—VIRTUALLY PERFECT
173—ABOUT LAST NIGHT...
224—FASCINATION*
229—FRICTION*
235—FLIRTATION*
267—HIDE & SEEK*
299—UNTOUCHED
343—PICK ME UP
365—TALKING IN YOUR SLEEP...
478—HARD TO RESIST**
498—CAUGHT IN THE ACT
542—MAKE YOUR MOVE

*The HotWires
**American Heroes

Don't miss any of our special offers. Write to us at the following address for information on our newest releases.

Harlequin Reader Service
U.S.: 3010 Walden Ave., P.O. Box 1325, Buffalo, NY 14269
Canadian: P.O. Box 609, Fort Erie, Ont. L2A 5X3

Happy holidays and Happy New Year to all of my readers, editors, to my agent, my husband, friends and family. I hope Santa treats all of you very well this year!

1

ABBY HARPER'S EYES clung to the man who stood not twenty feet away, dressed in an expensive silk suit that glided over his broad chest and muscled arms like water over rock.

Reece Winston.

She frowned, watching the restaurant hostess sidle up a little closer than necessary, making sure Reece had a clear view down the deep V of her low-cut blouse.

Abby couldn't blame her, not really, taking in the impressive figure Reece made as he turned, noticing the way the tailored pants clung to a perfect masculine ass that had her fingers itching to reach out for a squeeze.

She knew just how it would feel. She'd been there, done that.

Almost, anyway.

Once, a long, long time ago. How unfair—or pathetic—was it that she could remember the feel of one man's backside from eight years before?

To his credit, Reece barely seemed to notice the hostess, as he was deep in conversation with a small, hawkish man who stood beside him. Abby had heard Reece was home but hadn't seen him around, even though he lived next door.

That wasn't unusual. He'd come home a few times over the years since he'd left for life in Europe, but their paths had never intersected. She'd been off to school, or busy working at her parents' winery, and Reece had his life as a famous race car driver on the Formula One circuit. With the differences between their two lives, the half a mile between their homes might as well have been a thousand.

This was the first time she'd actually seen him anywhere but in a local newspaper or television sports report. Her heart beat a little too quickly for her liking. So she turned her attention away, though she wasn't really looking at the crowds milling around the Ithaca Commons, the artsy, outdoor shopping plaza in the heart of the small central New York city.

It was almost a month before Christmas, the Friday after Thanksgiving, which she had spent catching up on inventory. Abby and her friend Hannah were meeting here for lunch, something Abby had been looking forward to all week. Some downtime and a chance to forget about work for an hour or so.

Some light snow fell, blowing and circling around the booted feet of shoppers and local shopkeepers who were moving around the walkway. She hardly noticed. Her mind insisted on reminiscing about Reece.

She'd only kissed him once, on a crazy, wine-drenched evening one summer when he'd been home from college, the semester before he took off for Europe. They were both at the same lakeside party given by a mutual friend.

Even then, Reece ran with a crowd way out of Abby's league.

Abby had been seeing Josh Martin back then, a graduate student from Cornell Veterinary College who helped out at their vineyard, where they also hosted a small petting zoo with goats and sheep. Josh was a great guy. Cute.

Abby had been lying in wait by a dense hedgerow, intent on seducing her date. When she pulled the man she thought was Josh into the quiet, dark spot, she didn't give him a chance to say anything. She kissed him in clear invitation before he could say a word.

Abby discovered early on that she liked some kink with her sex, and Josh had a kind of quiet reserve that she took as a challenge. Sex outdoors at a party, with people right on the other side of the hedge, was an exciting thought for her, but she knew her mild-mannered date would have to be convinced.

She had pretty much made her way around second base heading for third when she told him how pleased she was with his sense of adventure and wondered what other experiments he might be up for.

Reece had chuckled softly and whispered in her ear that he would be happy to try anything she wanted to suggest.

She'd recognized his voice, and her mistake, immediately.

It had been *so* humiliating. Even now, her cheeks burned to think of it. She'd popped out from the hedges without even fixing her clothes, much to the amusement of some onlookers in the yard. Reece walked out, too, completely unapologetic with his shirt still unbuttoned, his eyes hot and the top button of his jeans undone. The button she had been undoing when he'd spoken up.

Worse, as furious as she was, she'd wanted to go back behind that hedge and finish what they'd started. Reece smiled and told her to lighten up, that he wouldn't have let it go too far. She imagined he and his buddies had a great laugh about it later.

Then he told her that Josh had received an emergency phone call and had to leave suddenly. Josh had asked Reece to find Abby and let her know. He'd started to say something else, but Abby had turned and left, and that was the last time she'd seen him, until now.

Reece had been her tormentor since childhood. The boy who always hid her lunchbox in the wrong locker, who tugged her pigtails and always, always rubbed it in that his parents' vineyards were bigger, more profitable and better than her family's smaller organic operation.

Though Reece teased her, he was never really mean. When she was fourteen, in fact, he defended her when another boy had been needlessly cruel about her braces, making her cry. Reece had almost punched the other boy, she remembered. Abby hated to admit it, but a secret, nasty little crush on him developed in that moment.

And he knew it.

And she knew that he knew, even when they both emerged back out from behind the hedge and he'd smiled at her so *knowingly*.

"Hey, earth to Abby?" The voice finally broke through as Hannah Morgan, her best friend since high school, returned to the table, sliding back into her seat.

Abby shook her head clear and blinked the past away.

"Sorry, lost in thought."

"Yeah, I saw Reece at the door. From the roses blooming in your cheeks, I assume you did, too."

Abby grunted. "It's just warm in here."

Hannah grinned widely. "Warmer since Reece walked in," she said without shame, watching him where he sat across the room from them. "I guess he's home because of what happened with his dad."

"I'm kind of surprised to see him, really. He had a bad crash last spring and has been recovering ever since—it was really serious," Abby said, shuddering as she remembered seeing the replay of the accident on the news. Reece had been on his way to superstardom, living a glamorous and high-profile life as a race car driver until the crash.

Hannah cocked an eyebrow. "I'd heard, but didn't realize you followed racing that closely."

"I just watch the news. And I might have read a few things online."

"Well, he looks healthy and hale to me," Hannah said with a playful leer.

Abby knew better than to look again, but did anyway, and sure enough, as soon as she peeked, Reece turned his head to look directly at her.

The shared look nearly sucked the breath out of her.

The years disappeared, and she was the crush-stricken teenager again. His eyes narrowed, and she knew that he recognized her, too, even though she was now twenty-five pounds lighter and her previously plain, boy-short brown hair was now long and layered, curling softly with honey-blond highlights, her one indulgence.

"Why does he have to be so *hot?*" Abby mumbled,

deeply annoyed and digging in to the beautiful salad that a server set before her moments ago. Shoving a forkful of spinach and various greens, fresh pears, walnuts and blue cheese into her mouth, she barely tasted it. Reece's fault.

"Hey, I think he's coming over," Hannah whispered across the table, looking up with a big smile as Reece approached them.

"What?" Abby sputtered, swallowing a mouthful of greens, promptly choking on her food as she saw Hannah was right. Abby coughed, reaching for her water, but suddenly strong hands had her from behind, spanning her rib cage and pulling her back against a rock-solid chest.

"I'm okay, I'm okay!" she insisted. She could sense the heat from his hands on her skin in spite of the sweater she wore over her blouse. His hold released, and she took a few breaths, composing herself.

"Abby?" he said in a voice that was deeper than she remembered, his breath just brushing the back of her neck.

She didn't turn around, not yet. Picking up her water, she took a sip, using the moment to focus. Then, smoothing the front of her sweater, she faced him with a bright smile.

"Reece. How nice to see you," she said, and was yet again flung back to those hedges as his gray eyes sparkled with warm recognition. He was remembering it, too, she could tell. Damn it. "Thanks for the first aid, but I really was okay," she said.

"Glad to help," he said. "So, Abby Harper, all grown

up. No more pigtails or braces," he said with a smile and a wink.

Her cheeks heated and she wanted to kick Hannah for grinning so broadly.

"I'm sorry to hear about your father. I hope he's doing well," Abby said, meaning it, determined to act like an adult.

She noticed a network of thin scars, recently healed, that ran along the side of his neck, and what looked like another behind his ear. "And you, too," she continued. "That was an awful accident they showed on the news. I'm so glad you're up and around. You look great," she said, proud of herself for sounding so mature, like an old friend who was happy to see him again.

Reece's expression became more serious. She thought he looked bigger now, more muscular than she remembered. She assumed that all race drivers kept to a rigorous fitness regimen and needed to be physically fit to withstand the physical and mental pressures of racing, but...wow.

Those beautiful, thick-lashed eyes were the same, as were the sharp cheekbones and full lips. She'd always loved how his pin-straight, raven-black hair had fallen in his eyes, a little long in the front, but now he kept it cropped short, which only accented his features all the more.

"Thank you. Dad's recovering well. Doctors are very optimistic."

He obviously didn't want to discuss his own near miss, and she couldn't say she blamed him. Regardless of his celebrity status, it couldn't be fun to have your private life and health problems made into entertainment news.

Abby nodded. "Is he still at the hospital? I imagine he'd probably be happy to be back to work when he can."

Reece frowned. "Actually, he won't. The surgery was remarkably fast—they can do amazing things these days. He and Mom were only home for a few days, but they're down with Ben now, in South Carolina. The doctors advised it, so that he'd be in an easier climate, closer to hospitals. They'll live with Ben and his family for a while, which will make it easier on Mom. Then they plan to find a new place down there."

"Oh," she said, her reaction part surprise and part regret. She liked the Winstons and would have liked to have seen them before they left. They'd been good neighbors. "Who's taking over the vineyards? You?"

It was what she'd done when her parents retired. They were off catching up on all of the travel they had put off all those years. Abby was happy for them and she loved the updates they sent her and posted on their Facebook pages. Her parents—world adventurers.

"Not exactly," Reece said, looking cautious. "We've decided selling is the best option. I'm taking care of the details, though, and I have some buyers interested, but—"

"You're selling?" she interrupted, in shock.

"Yes, I'm afraid so."

"But, I thought…now that you're not racing…"

Her misstep was reflected in the tightening of his expression.

"I want to be back to racing next year," he said shortly.

"As soon as possible, really. So there's no choice but to sell. Which reminds me," he said, glancing over at his table, "I have to get back to my meeting. I just wanted to say hello."

"Oh," was all Abby managed to say.

Reece's expression shifted from cool to friendly again. Maybe a little too smoothly, in Abby's estimation.

"It's good to see you, though. Maybe we'll get a chance to have a drink together over the holiday, catch up on old times. I should be home for the month, to see the sale through and finish things up here," he said.

"Yeah, sure," she responded, but he'd already turned to walk away. This time, she did notice a slight hitch in his gait and wondered about his injuries. Things might be happening behind the scenes that the public didn't know about…still, she'd thought from what had been reported in the news and online that he was out of the sport.

"Wow, I can't believe he's selling," Abby said again, her mind returning to that bombshell. There were some new start-ups along the lake, and some of the vineyards had closed over the years, but Maple Hills and Winston Vineyards were the two oldest in the area. "All the news said he was out of racing. His accident left him with injuries that simply won't allow him back in."

"He seems to think differently," Hannah said absently.

Abby watched Reece sit down at his table and then turned to see Hannah worriedly chewing her lip.

"What?"

"I hope he hasn't been talking with the Keller Corp.

rep. The same guy who bought out Stevens and Harvest vineyards last year."

Abby put her fork back down, her hands turning cold.

"No."

"It's a possibility."

"He…can't. He can't sell to them. It would ruin Maple Hills!" As if selling wasn't bad enough, selling to Keller would be a disaster.

Keller was a housing developer that had been buying up lakeside property and building cookie-cutter housing developments that ruined the area's natural appeal. They didn't care about the watershed or about the long tradition of wineries in the area. They didn't care about anything, except for making money.

The runoff from pavement, lawn chemicals and the potential for septic leaks and so forth, would be awful for her business, ruining her land. Not to mention scarring the beautiful view of the lake.

"Every wedding couple we book wants to be married out on the vineyard, with the view of the lake. We'd lose them all if the backdrop is a bunch of prefab houses," she said, shaking her head.

Even in the economic hard times, people still got married, and these days many of them decided to do so locally to save money. Her wedding bookings were up considerably, and that helped when wine sales were down. In fact, she was preparing for a wedding reception that was scheduled for two days before Christmas. Weddings and other special events had become a big part of her bottom line.

Harvey Winston, Reece's father, hadn't been an

organic farmer, not strictly, but he used the least harmful methods available and made sure to observe a buffer between her grapes and his. And all of the vineyards worked to maintain the beauty of the landscape, as it was to their collective advantage.

No way would Keller Corp. care. In fact, if they drove her out, they would buy up her family business, as well.

"He can't do it, Hannah."

"Well, he can, sadly. And probably will if he wants to sell fast and for a good price," Hannah said flatly, making Abby sit back in her chair, utterly losing her appetite altogether.

"There has to be some other way. I should talk to him, maybe we can work something out."

"I'm sorry, hon, but I do your accounting, and there is no way you can afford to buy him out. Speaking as your friend, without Sarah, you already have more than you can manage alone. Maybe if you hire someone…" Hannah said sympathetically.

"I planned to, in the summer. I don't have time for interviews now. But if he sells, none of it will matter."

Sarah had been her manager and her second-in-command. She'd known the winery and their vineyards inside out, had been with them since her parents ran the place, but finally had also decided to retire a few months before. It had been tough finding a suitable replacement. Abby had been running in circles handling everything.

"What are you thinking?" she asked Hannah, who had that look that told Abby her friend was clearly cooking up something as she smiled mysteriously.

"Well, he was awfully eager to get his hands on you—no way were you choking badly enough for him to jump in and Heimlich you."

"What are you saying?"

"I'm saying you two always had some chemistry, always had a little push and pull between you. Maybe that's something you could use to your advantage."

"You're deluded."

"You know it's true. You said yourself that he was a great kisser and you wish that snafu behind the hedgerow had gone further. So…"

"No fair. I said that when I was really drunk."

"And we know alcohol is like truth serum for you. But why not give it a try?"

"Are you seriously suggesting I sleep with Reece in order to get him to change his mind about selling?"

"I wouldn't put it that way. Just…strike up your old friendship, flirt a little, see if you can make him more sympathetic to your cause. Or at the very least, keep your enemies closer so you know what's going on. He seemed interested in meeting up for a drink, and well, it can't hurt, right?"

Abby narrowed her eyes. "I don't believe I've seen this side of your personality. Very *Desperate Housewives.* But it's not for me. Besides, that incident behind the bushes was a mistake. Before that, the only chemistry we had was him tormenting me since second grade."

"Boys always punch girls in the arm when they like them."

"You've been watching *Brady Bunch* repeats again, haven't you?" Abby accused, and both of them collapsed in laughter for a moment, before Abby sighed, sobering again.

"I'm afraid we'll have to come up with some other plan."

"Maybe it's for the best," Hannah suggested. "I know the developments suck, but you haven't had a vacation in almost two years, and have you even been out on a date in that time?"

"One," Abby challenged.

Though that hadn't been so much of a date as a disaster.

"All you do is work. Your parents never meant for you to have no life when they turned the place over. Maybe if you sold it, you could—"

Abby looked at her in horror. "How can you even say that? My parents risked everything, worked their entire lives to make this business a success, and at a time when organic farming had hardly been heard of, let alone been popular. How can I just sell out on them?"

Hannah shrugged. "It's worth thinking about, from a practical perspective, hon. Things change. Sometimes you have to change with them."

Abby knew she had been working too hard, almost constantly since Sarah retired, and Hannah was right on one score—as her parents' only child, they were delighted to give her the business, but they were also huge believers in balance. They would be the first ones to tell her to ease up—yet they would also never sell to somebody like Keller, Abby knew that in her heart of hearts.

There had to be some way she could talk to Reece, find an alternative or get him to change his mind. Short of sleeping with him, not that the idea didn't have some appeal. He was gorgeous, undeniably.

"I guess I could at least talk to him," she said lamely, watching Reece deep in conversation with his business associate over big sandwiches. Thinking about those strong hands on her rib cage and the hot kisses they had shared, she wondered if Hannah wasn't on to something.

Maybe her friend was right. Why not? They were old friends—sort of—but they were both grown up now. She hadn't had so much as a kiss good-night in months. She knew for a fact that kissing Reece wouldn't be any sacrifice at all, and if it would get him to listen to her...

All of her appetites kicked back in, and with a dash of hope she dug back into her salad.

Hannah's lips twitched and she had a self-satisfied look. "You're thinking about it, aren't you?"

Abby couldn't resist a smile. "Hey, you're the one who wants me to go out on a date. Besides, it's not like I would let it go too far," she said, echoing Reece's words from so long ago. "I wouldn't trade sex for him selling the place to me or anything tawdry like that, but as you said, maybe just some flirting, spending time together, might help him see my side of things a little better."

"Exactly. Just be careful. Remember from eleventh-grade chemistry what happens when you put two volatile substances together," Hannah warned, but her eyes were twinkling with mischief.

"Maybe," Abby said, but her mind was racing ahead, intrigued by the idea of flirting with Reece. "But what a way to go."

REECE WAS HAVING a hard time focusing, and it had nothing to do with the injuries he'd sustained nine months before and everything to do with the unbelievably sexy woman sitting across the room. He could hardly believe that was Abby Harper.

Seeing her had been the first pleasant surprise he'd had since coming back to help with his family's affairs. Life had been one long string of disasters for the past year. First, two members of his racing team had to be replaced at the start of the season, after which they'd lost a major sponsor, and then he'd had his accident at the end of March, right when he'd been about to turn a major corner in his career.

Everyone told him he was lucky to be alive and in one piece, walking and talking again, and he supposed that was true. He'd been in a coma for three days, followed by six months of language and physical therapy after he had emerged from the coma, his head injury leaving him with a broken memory and speech problems. He'd overcome it all. Mostly.

Some of the guys he'd known hadn't made it through crashes that left them with lesser injuries, but there were a lot of days when Reece didn't feel all that lucky, especially since they told him there would be no more racing, not until a neurologist cleared him. Then his dad had a major heart attack. It had been one thing after another, and Reece found his time split between his recovery and wanting to get back to racing and having to help out his family. They'd been there for him, and there was no way he'd leave them in the lurch now, but it sure didn't make things easier. His life was an ocean away.

For months his mom and dad had been traveling back

and forth to Europe, where Reece lived just outside of Paris. It was too much strain for them to try to run the winery and travel so often, and his father's illness was proof of that. He felt responsible, and although they'd bent over backward to tell him it wasn't his fault, guilt demanded he stay here and help in any way he could.

He'd been here, in central New York State, for a few weeks, though he had spent most of the time at the hospital, in hotels and then getting his parents to his brother's home down South. He couldn't help the feeling that his real life was passing him by. He could only be absent from racing for so long. There were always new guys coming up, ready to take his place, and sponsors had short memories. Few drivers came back after a crash like his; hell, few survived.

But Reece wasn't ready to retire yet. He just had to sell the winery, to do the best he could by his parents and get back to France ASAP. At thirty-one, he didn't have too many years left to get back into the game.

Though some guys raced into their forties, it was getting to be less and less the case, so he needed to still show he could do the job. The doctors were apprehensive, but he planned to prove them wrong. He'd come this far, he was going the rest of the way.

He thought again of Abby's shocked face when he'd said he was going to sell the winery. His parents weren't thrilled, either, but they'd long ago accepted that both of their boys had other lives now. Still, Reece was bothered by the clear disapproval in Abby's gorgeous brown eyes when he'd made the announcement.

"So, I can bring the Keller representative by tomorrow, if you like," Charles said.

Charles Tyler was one of the premiere real estate agents in the area, and he was also a shark—if anyone could sell the place for the best price, it would be him.

"They'd be a last resort. I thought I made that clear."

Charles sighed, smiling slightly at the pretty server who delivered their lunch. "Well, if you want it sold for the asking price and fast, they are the best bet. They'll jump at a property as large as yours."

Reece frowned. They'd also tear down the renovated farmhouse he grew up in, and they'd flatten the vineyards, rows of Riesling, Chardonnay and Pinot Noir grapes, paving them over with cul-de-sacs and driveways. He'd been away, but he kept in touch, and he'd seen the changes along the lake since he'd come back, few of them good.

"Some of those vines have been around longer than my parents have been alive, planted by my grandfather," Reece murmured, not realizing he'd said it out loud.

"Well, you might be able to sell to another winery, but it won't go for nearly as much, not in this economic climate," Charles said with a sigh, no doubt disappointed that sentimentality could get in the way of a larger commission for him. "And it could take quite a bit longer."

Reece nodded, thinking. "Keep Keller on the line, but let's not move too fast. If they want it now, they'll want it a month from now, but let's see what comes up in the meanwhile," he said, his eyes drifting back to Abby.

"Who's the girl?" Charles asked, following Reece's gaze.

"Abby Harper. An old friend, her family owns the winery next to ours, Maple Hills."

"More than a friend?" Charles asked.

"No. Just a girl I knew in high school," Reece said.

"Any chance she might be interested in selling, as well? I could get you a sweet deal if you two went in on a sale together—that could significantly up the price Keller would offer."

"I doubt she would ever sell, and definitely not to Keller," Reece said.

"They're not the devil," Charles said dryly. "They just build developments, nice ones, which tend to fill up very quickly."

"I know what they do," Reece said absently, his attention still on Abby.

Charles picked up the check and changed the subject, droning on about local real estate markets or some other big sale he had just completed, all of which Reece tuned out.

Abby was in close conversation with her friend, whom he only vaguely remembered from school. He and Abby hadn't really belonged to the same crowd, even though they grew up next door to each other and shared a common interest between their families.

Her folks were always a little different than everyone else on the lake—more iconoclastic, with their organic methods and sustainable farming beliefs, the petting zoo and homespun lifestyle. Those things were all the rage now, of course. Maple Hills could ask twice for a bottle of wine what other noncertified organic vineyards could.

While they were still primarily a small family business, Maple Hills had broadened its distribution and marketing quite successfully in recent years, so his father said. Probably Abby's doing. She had a good head for business and was growing it well.

She'd taken a lot of ribbing in school—she and her parents being called hippies and so forth—and quite a bit of that had been from him. He hadn't meant any of it, not in a mean-spirited way, but even then, Abby had been fun to tease. He could never resist.

Her cheeks turned pink if he even looked at her, and he's always thought it was cute. He'd never suspected she would be as hot and as daring as he had discovered that night at the lake party.

It was the last time he'd seen her until now. Though he'd kissed plenty of women in between—including a few A-list celebrities—the memory of Abby Harper pressed up against him and kissing him for all she was worth, her hands everywhere, was as clear to him as if it had happened five minutes ago.

He'd wanted to drag her back behind the hedge that night, and he'd regretted making light of it afterward. She'd bolted before he could ask her out. On a date. So they could do it right.

He wanted to make up for what he'd been too much of an immature idiot to do in high school. He'd always liked her, but when he was young, he was too worried about what his friends would think. Typical teenage boy stuff.

A few years later, on that night by the lake, he didn't care what anyone thought, but Abby was clearly not interested as soon as she found out whom she'd been feeling up behind the bushes.

He'd known, in some corner of his mind, that she hadn't been in real danger of choking at her table earlier, but seeing her had somehow led to the immediate need to touch her. He'd become semihard from the way her pretty backside pressed against him when he'd been trying to help her, his wrists just brushing the undersides of her full breasts when he'd wrapped his arms around her.

Sad, when emergency Heimlich was your excuse to get close to a woman, but Reece hadn't had sex since before his accident and, apparently, his body was more than ready for some action. Despite lingering effects from his injuries, that part of his nervous system seemed to be in fine working order.

What if he decided to pursue that drink with Abby and see if they could pick up where they'd left off by the bushes? She hadn't been interested back then, but he could swear he'd felt her respond to his touch today, and not just in a panic about choking.

It was fun to think about, and it might be worth seeing the look on her face if he asked. He couldn't resist the idea of teasing Abby, even now, though the way he wanted to tease her had taken on a whole new dimension.

He chuckled to himself, feeling better than he had in weeks.

"Something funny about that?" Charles asked, obviously peeved, either because he knew Reece wasn't listening, or because Reece had just laughed at something he shouldn't have.

"Oh, no, sorry. I was just thinking about something else," he said vaguely.

"Okay, well, I'll start pushing the property and see what we can do to hold Keller off for a while, but unless you want to wait longer, they may be the best deal in town," Charles repeated.

"I'll talk to them, but I just want to see what other offers we get. I'll be living at the house, so you can get me there. You have my numbers," Reece said.

"I'll do my best." Charles stood and shook Reece's hand firmly, an action that sent a buzz of numbness rushing up his arm, making him wince and reminding him all of the problems from his accident that still remained.

The short-lived nerve reaction ticked off a bit of desperation, nearly making him tell Charles to sell to Keller now. Reece had to get back to Europe, had to get better and had to race again. It was the only life he knew or wanted.

But Charles was on his way out, and Reece took a breath, calming down. It would be okay. He'd healed faster than anyone thought he would, and he'd be on the track again before next summer. Still, the sooner he could conclude his business here, the better, he thought with a small pang of regret as he took one more glimpse of Abby before leaving the café.

2

The next day, Abby was busy from the moment she woke up, barely able to keep up with everything she had to get done, even though it was a weekend. Weekends—Saturdays, anyway—were busier than weekdays for her, and today was no exception.

She'd waited all morning only to be stood up by an electrician who was supposed to show up during the week, but had rescheduled and then stood her up again. Some overhead lights kept flickering intermittently in the main room of the winery, and she needed it fixed yesterday.

Today they'd had three tastings and tours offered at ten o'clock, noon and two, and in between that she was fielding online orders, wedding prep and Christmas decorating that should have been done two weeks ago. The guests were fewer than they had been over the summer, or on holidays like Valentine's Day, when they did their wine-and-chocolate parties. Still, they'd had a respectable showing for each tour.

Right now she was in the middle of the last tasting, and while she was exhausted, her mind running in a million directions, she focused on smiling, explaining the type and origin of each wine and its story.

All of their wines had stories, background about how old the vines were, where they came from, who planted them and anything fun or anecdotal that happened while the wine was being made. It personalized the experience and made people aware that the wine they sipped wasn't just any generic wine, but a drink with a specific history, made by real people.

"This peppery Baco Noir," she said, finishing her presentation, "is called 'Just the Beginning' and it is one of our classic vintages. One summer night almost forty years ago, two lovers walked over the fields behind us, and the man asked the woman he was with to marry him. They didn't have enough money for rings, but he handed her a small plant, the beginning of the Baco vines from which these grapes still grow. Those people were my parents and, yes, eventually he did buy her a ring," Abby said warmly, smiling as she did every time she told the story.

A chorus of appreciative comments and chuckles about the ring followed. She discussed nuances, taught newcomers the basics of wine tasting and then moved to the desk where people purchased their wine and other goodies from the small gift display.

It was a good day, and she'd enjoyed her guests. By six, though, she was ready for bed. Her other employees were gone for the day, and they rarely had guests staying in their few upstairs rooms, used mostly for wedding parties in the winter. So, she closed up shop and thought of what needed to be done next.

She did need to get the trees decorated—three gorgeous Fraser firs that graced the tasting room, the entry to the winery and the first floor of the main house. Her home, a private residence, was built off the central rooms where they hosted tastings, receptions and sold their wines. In the back of the property, above the vineyards, were the animal barns and the building where they made and stored the wines. Their specialty was Baco Noir.

The trees were set up, the lights were on, but they needed ornaments, all of which had to be pulled out of storage at the house and carried over. She also needed to take care of her horses for the night.

They no longer had the petting zoo, unfortunately, but Abby could never part with her horses. Riding them along the lake was one of her favorite ways to relax. Her parents had given her these two colts when she was fifteen. As she headed down to the barn and looked out over her land, the sight always took her breath away in any season. Today, there'd been a light snow all day long, and it was shining like diamonds in the moonlight.

This was hers. It was home. Like her parents, she'd love to travel more, but she'd never really wanted to live anywhere but here.

All of the stress and work that went with it was hers, too. Lunch with Hannah yesterday had left her with a lot of food for thought and a lot of worry for the future.

Inside the barn she was greeted by soft, muffled welcomes, and she grabbed feed buckets, hay and fresh water and took care of business, which included much brushing and stroking.

"Hey, babes," she crooned, feeling guilty that she hadn't done more than put them out in the field that day. "I promise tomorrow you'll both get some good exercise. I'll get Hannah and we'll see you both early in the morning for a nice ride."

After long moments of petting warm muzzles and feeling more relaxed than she had when she walked in, she locked the doors and said good-night, turning back toward the house. Her gaze drifted down over the landscape to the Winston property. She noted some lights on in the house, although the winery was dark. Was Reece really going to sell?

She shivered, pulled her thick wool coat tighter around her and stared at the upstairs light. Reece? In his room? Was he there alone? She shivered for a different reason.

She'd been all fired up yesterday, having fun with Hannah, but she was crazy to think she could seduce Reece into…what? Not selling his land? No doubt he would think that was very funny; she was still out of his league, always had been.

But she *was* going to talk to him. She had no idea what she'd say to try to convince him to hold off, but if he didn't rush into a sale with Keller, maybe she could help find someone who would buy in with her. It was a huge gambit, but not impossible. Not entirely. She had money saved, and she'd have to mortgage her home to the hilt, but what other choice did she have?

She had to do whatever she could to protect her home and business. Keller would ruin the entire area.

The little hamlet that had sprouted up around the wineries a few miles up the lake from the city of Ithaca offered a coffee shop, a few quaint boutiques, a gas station and a convenience store, and all of her friends were here. Unlike Reece, who had gone away as far as he could as soon as he was able, she'd gone to college locally, at Cornell, and she went down into the city a few times a week. They sold many of their wines in local stores, as well as all over the region.

She wished she could go inside, open a nice bottle of wine, make some dinner and sit in front of the fireplace in the living room, then finish decorating her trees without it feeling like work.

It would be even nicer to not have to do it alone.

Maybe she wouldn't have to. Biting her lip, she walked faster toward the house and didn't think too much about what she was contemplating. If she did, she'd lose her nerve.

Entering the warmly lit kitchen that hadn't changed too much since she'd grown up, she went carefully down the cellar steps to the room where they kept their private stock and grabbed a bottle she had been saving for a special occasion.

Back upstairs, she pulled two glasses from the shelves and a wedge of brie and a few other goodies from the fridge.

The trees could wait. Her talk with Reece could not.

If she didn't do it now, she'd could lose her chance as well as her nerve. Setting aside her doubts and worries, she started out walking across the land between their homes, a windy half mile, her eyes focused on the lit windows. The snow and moon illuminated everything, making it easy to walk, and she covered the distance quickly. As she neared the house, her eyes focused in on a form in the upstairs window.

Her mouth went dry and she dropped the bottle of wine, which didn't break, thank goodness, but landed softly in the snow.

She picked it up again and walked closer. It was Reece. He hadn't pulled a shade or a curtain, thinking—rightly—that no one would be looking in his windows from the field side of the house.

He was nude. Completely. Stretching his arms up over his head, and then bending at the waist, she couldn't see everything, but she saw enough to make her heart slam against her rib cage as he did something that looked very much like yoga.

He was strong. Muscled, but graceful in his movements.

Gorgeous.

She forgot to move forward, entranced, but then as she realized where she was and what she was doing, she averted her eyes—though she couldn't erase what she'd seen. How could she? The strong line of his back, the muscles of his shoulders and arms were stunning. She could imagine running her hands over him and wondered what it would be like to have those slim, strong hips settling in between her legs.…

"Oh, no," she said to herself, breathless with lust, her hands trembling as she almost dropped the wine again.

She hovered for a second on the porch. Reece was home, alone and naked, and she was standing here at his front door with a bottle of wine. Her courage flagged. Maybe she should talk to him another time, like during the light of day, or at a bar with a lot of other people around.

Don't be a coward, Abby, she scolded herself. She sucked in a deep breath and pressed the doorbell before she could change her mind.

REECE STEPPED GINGERLY out of the shower, wrapping a large towel around his waist, wincing from the pain in his left leg, where pins and needles shot back and forth along his thigh, causing weakness in his stance.

Each pinprick was like an individual jab, reminding him that he couldn't get in a race car again and do the thing that he loved most. Headaches had come back earlier that afternoon as well, and he'd spent most of the day on the sofa with an ice pack.

What if this never went away? What if they never signed off on letting him race again? At this point, doctors gave him a fifty-fifty shot, but he had to be one hundred percent, his reflexes perfect, completely reliable before he could race.

The betrayal of having his own body prevent him from doing what he loved most was utterly unacceptable. He'd gotten through the worst of it, and he'd defeat this, too. There was no alternative other than…what? Staying here?

Not an option.

Crossing the hall, he walked into the guest room and dried off. His mother had long ago, with his blessing, turned his old room into a place where she did her sewing and other crafts. He came home for holidays and a few short vacations but not often enough for his parents to have preserved his room. At the moment, he was glad they hadn't. He'd been feeling strangely sentimental about the old place, and that wasn't like him. He supposed it was because of the close call with his dad. Almost losing someone—as well as almost losing your own life—made you see things differently.

He loved his family, but this was just a house, he reminded himself. A building. One he couldn't get away from fast enough when he'd been a teenager looking for something more exciting.

He started going through the stretching routine that he'd been taught by his last physical therapist to relieve the pins and needles. Focusing on his breathing, his form, he drove away unwanted thoughts. The hot shower had helped loosen him up, but it still hurt like hell at first to push through the moves and hold them, though the symptoms lessened after a few repetitions.

He felt better as he relaxed, going through the rest of his exercises for good measure. He'd talked to his neurologist earlier in the day for the umpteenth time, and he had been reassured yet again that it was all normal.

Easy for him to say.

Reece turned to grab a pair of jeans when the ring of the doorbell caught him by surprise. Who would be here now?

Surely not Charles with someone to see the house. No one had called.

Pulling on his jeans and grabbing a shirt, he rushed down the stairs and pulled open the door, unable to believe his eyes.

"Abby?"

He took in her pink cheeks and tousled hair, and stepped back, inviting her in as the frosty air nipped at his bare toes.

"C'mon in. It's freezing out there," he said.

"Thanks, it is," she said, moving quickly. Her eyes flew to his chest. He hadn't had time to completely button his shirt.

"Oh, sorry…just got out of the shower."

Her cheeks turned even pinker and she didn't meet his eyes. He wondered why she was here holding wine, two glasses and some other foods.

Reece prompted her again. "What's all this?" he asked, looking down at the stuff she still held in her arms. One glass was tenuously dangling from her fingertips.

"Let me take that for you," he offered, and reached forward to take the flute. When his fingers caught with hers around the stem, her hand jerked away and they fumbled the glass, nearly dropping the fragile crystal.

Reece frowned. "Are you okay?"

She finally smiled. "Yes, I'm fine. Sorry to intrude on your evening, but I saw your lights on and felt like some company. You said you wanted to have a drink, so…" She shrugged, holding up the bottle. "Unless this is a bad time?"

He remembered saying something about having a drink when he'd seen her at the restaurant. This wasn't exactly what he meant, but maybe it was better.

He'd had a rough day, and having a bottle of wine with a pretty woman might be exactly what he needed.

"It's a perfect time, actually. I'm really glad you decided to stop by," he said, smiling and taking the rest of the things she was holding so that she could shuck her jacket. "You walked all the way over, in the dark?"

"It wasn't that dark, with the snow and the moon.

Very nice, actually," she said lightly, handing him her coat just as she met his eyes and a spark flared as his hand touched hers.

She shifted uncomfortably, looking away and turning pink again. Reece didn't remember her being so... wait.

She'd come across the field on the side of the house where the guest room was. Where he'd been doing his stretching, with the curtains open. With no clothes on. He never closed the drapes, since no one was likely to be lurking out in the fields

Silence hung at the end of her comment, and he had to smother a smile. She had to have seen him. Reece wasn't shy and had to resist the urge to tease her about it.

So Abby was bit of a voyeur? It didn't bother him. He'd be happy to let her look all she liked, he thought, his grin breaking loose as he turned away to hang her coat.

Maybe this evening would go even better than he thought.

"Grab that bottle and we can go put the food together in the kitchen, then sit by the fire," he said casually, though he wasn't feeling casual at all. All of his worries were pushed back by a surge of unexpected lust, and it felt great. He wanted to hold on to it, ride it and see where it took him.

"Oh, that would be nice," she said, walking with him to the kitchen. Dressed in jeans and a sweater that accentuated her curves, he leaned forward and pulled something from her hair. He could swear she sucked in a breath when he did, becoming perfectly still.

Hmm.

He presented a straw of hay to her with a smile. "Been down with your horses, I take it?"

She rolled her eyes and snatched the hay from his hand, but couldn't hold back a laugh, which made her even prettier. He'd always thought she was pretty, even as a little girl, but now…she was incredible. She always looked so natural and fresh, and he wondered what her skin tasted like.

"Yes, I was closing them up for the night when I saw your lights on my way back from the barn."

"Do you still have just the two? Buttercup and Beau?"

She paused, looking surprised that he remembered. He was a little surprised, too.

"Yes. Wow, you know their names," she said bluntly, taking the plate he handed her to open the brie so they could heat it up in the small toaster oven he pointed to.

"Why so surprising? We went to the same school, rode the same bus," he said. "Must've just stuck in my mind, I guess."

"Huh. I didn't think you knew I was alive unless you were poking at me about something," she said, and it was his turn to be a little surprised.

"I always liked you. I teased you, sure, but did you feel like I picked on you? Really?" A small frown creased his lips. He didn't like thinking he had hurt Abby's feelings or been mean to her.

Taking the food, they made their way to the main room and set the dishes down on the coffee table, placing a platter with green grapes, crackers and apples and the warmed brie between them. All perfect to go with the Baco, but Reece waited for her answer before moving to the fire.

She looked him in the eye and sighed lightly. "Well, you have to admit, aside from teasing me or pulling my hair, you didn't give me reason to think you knew I existed, let alone that you would remember details of my life."

"Hmm," he said thoughtfully, rubbing his chin slowly. "I remember some things very clearly," he said with a teasing wink.

"You can't even resist now, can you?" she said accusingly, but a smile twitched at her lips.

She remembered what happened between them that night at the lake as clearly as he did, he'd bet. And, no, he wasn't sure he could resist, or wanted to. But there was time. He backed away, letting it drop for now.

"Let me put a few more logs on the fire and we can eat. Suddenly I'm starving."

He was, though he wasn't sure the food on the plate was what he had a taste for, but it would have to be enough for the moment.

They spent the next two hours eating and talking in front of the crackling fire, when Abby suddenly looked around the room.

"You don't have a tree or any Christmas decorations up," she observed.

He shrugged. "There hasn't been any time, or much point, I guess. I'm the only one here, and Charles, the real estate agent, thought it was better to show the place without a lot of decorations. Let people imagine their own lives here and all that."

"Oh," she remarked, her expression turning serious. "That's kind of what I wanted to talk to you about," she said carefully.

"Christmas decorations?"

"No, that you're selling. I was hoping—"

Reece put a hand up. "Abby, I'd be happy to sit down and talk business with you at some point. But not right now, okay?"

"But—"

"It's been kind of a tough day. I'd really like to relax, catch up with an old friend," he said.

He geniunely didn't want to talk business with Abby. He knew she'd want to convince him not to sell, or something like that, and he didn't want to discuss that with her. It was a done deal, and that conversation was sure to put a damper on the heat building between them.

She bit her lip and looked reluctant, but nodded. "I can understand that," she said, looking down at her wine. "I know things must have been hard for you this year," she said vaguely, inviting him to say more, but he didn't want to talk about any of that, either. Maybe that wasn't fair, but he needed a night off from all of it.

"Yeah," he said, and changed the subject. "But how about you? You live in the house alone now?"

Nothing like discreet fishing before you tried to seduce an old friend, he thought. Hopefully there wasn't another guy in the picture, though looking at her, it was hard to believe they weren't lined up.

She shook her head, and his relief was immediate.

"Nope, just me now. Sarah retired, and Mom and

Dad are traveling all over the world. I still have a small part-time staff, of course, to help me get things done, but I handle most of it myself."

"They don't come home for the holidays? Your parents?"

"It would be difficult. They send gifts, and we video conference on the computer a lot. Last year they were in India, helping local people build a school. This winter, they've been helping down in Haiti."

"Really? I thought they were tourists now?"

"They mix their pleasure travel with activism. It's just their way, and they have always been more like explorers than tourists."

He nodded, smiling. "I remember."

"I know what they're doing is important, and I'm a big girl. We're busy enough through the holidays that being alone at Christmas gives me a quiet day or two to relax, read, sleep in, that kind of thing."

"Your parents were always so progressive," he said admiringly, but really he was thinking about Abby sleeping in, under the covers, warm and soft, curled up in something slinky with a book. Then he imagined taking the book out of her hands and slipping the lacy bit of nothing from her shoulder....

"Reece?" she said, and he realized he had gone blank, lost in his fantasy. "Are you okay?"

She seemed worried, and it bothered him. Of all the people he didn't want worrying if he was healthy and ready to go, she was first on the list at the moment.

"Sorry. You just made me remember that summer when your parents decided to try to add selling goat cheese to the winery business, and all of the goats got loose one weekend and ate some of my dad's vines," he lied, unable to look away from her face. Her eyes had landed on the scar behind his ear—the skin graft had healed, but it was visible. Did it bother her?

The definite sparkle of interest in her eyes said no, he assumed.

She laughed then, breaking the bond. "He was pretty nice about it, considering."

Her honey-brown hair was soft and slightly curled, pushed back in a haphazard way that made him want to reach out and weave his hands into it. She didn't wear makeup, which he found refreshing. She didn't need to. Her skin was flawless, her cheeks pink and kissable. And those lips…

"Did you ever wonder?" he heard himself ask.

Her cheeks turned rosy again, her lips parting slightly, as if she knew exactly where his mind had gone.

"Wonder what?"

He paused. They'd had a nice evening, two old friends talking over high school times and getting reacquainted. Did he really want to step into other waters? He was only back for a month or so, or however long it took to sell the winery. And the faster, the better. Abby wasn't one of his pit stops.

The women he knew in Europe were aware of his commitment-free lifestyle, his focus on his racing. They knew the score. They also had their own agendas, liking to be seen with a well-known driver, having their picture show up in the next day's entertainment news.

Abby had no agenda. She was just…Abby.

He still had to ask the question.

"What it might have been like if we didn't stop that night at the lake?" he said and noted the slight catch in her breath, but she didn't look away.

"Sure, I wondered," she said simply.

"I was about to ask you out, back then, when you took off," he admitted.

"You were?"

"Yeah. I wanted to know what it would be like to be with you, for real," he said. "I always liked you, Abby. A lot."

"Oh" was her only response, sounding slightly breathless. He took that as a good sign and plunged ahead.

"Still want to find out?" he said, in spite of every bit of better judgment he had.

Her eyes widened in surprise and she stood suddenly, setting down her wine, her movements fluttering and nervous.

"I should go. We're just tired. There's the fire and the wine, and it's easy to be caught up in old times, but really…I should go," she repeated, and walked to the door.

Reece shot up, moving after her.

"I'm sorry," he said, catching her arm, turning her to him. "I didn't mean to scare you off."

He wasn't sure if he was talking about eight years ago or two minutes ago. He was sure he didn't want her walking out the door.

They were close, and she looked up at him, her eyes somber.

"Listen, Reece, as much as I might be…curious, too, it wouldn't be a good idea—"

"You're curious?" His mind selectively honed in on

the one thing he wanted to hear and he stepped closer. "About me?"

She licked her lips nervously, making his cock jerk, semihard already, against the rough fabric of his jeans. In his hurry, he hadn't even pulled on briefs, so all that held him back was a bit of thin fabric.

"I—" She had started to say something, but he saw the pulse beating hard at the base of her throat, the desire in her eyes.

"What else are you curious about, Abby? I seem to remember you liked the excitement of being there, by the hedge, in public. Are you still up for that kind of adventure?"

He remembered how aroused she had been, and it had been just as hot for him, too. Did she still want that?

Reece liked risk, too. Hell, it defined him. He also had fantasies that not all of his lovers had satisfied.

What kind of sex was Abby into? He knew about her fondness for public places. Bondage, maybe? Something more creative? Role-play, perhaps?

He wanted to find out, imagining Abby tied to his bed or dressed in black leather. What if she wanted him tied up?

He could probably live with that. He was open to anything short of real pain or multiple partners—Reece wasn't sharing Abby with anyone.

"Let's just see, Abby, what it could be like between us," he said, needing to know and pulling her to him, his hands traveling up her back and into her hair, as he'd thought about.

It was like silk. He wanted to feel it trailing over his stomach and his thighs, her mouth on him.

The thought made his kiss less introductory, less tentative, than it might have been otherwise. He took her soft lips and opened her wider, invading and rubbing his tongue against hers with a deep moan. She felt so right, like she had before, but better, the flames leaping between them.

Her arms went around his neck, and she rubbed back with her tongue, her lips and the rest of her body as she strained against him.

Green flag, he thought, but resisted accelerating, instead maintaining the steady heat of the kiss, learning her taste, her touch, until neither of them could take it any longer.

When her hands started undoing the buttons on his shirt, he walked her back against the wall by the window, pressing his hardness against her, moving his hands up to cover her breasts. She was firm and soft in his palms, the nipples budding hard.

Touching wasn't enough, he needed to taste.

Moving his hands up under her sweater, he set the flimsy lace of her bra aside and bent to take one tight, beaded nipple in his mouth. He drew on it hard, murmuring encouragingly as she arched away from the wall, her hand at the back of his head, keeping him there.

He replaced his lips with his fingers, rolling the warm buds between his thumb and forefinger as he kissed her again, wanting to be everywhere at once.

He stood back, staring down into her flushed face, her passion-drenched eyes, raising a finger to touch lips that now looked like crushed cherries.

"Abby, I want you, but…" He let the question hang. He wanted her, but he'd back off now if she wanted him to, no matter what.

"Yes, please," she said, her breathing short and hard.

She was incredibly sweet. He planned to take his time with her, he thought, and pressed her back, sliding a thigh between her legs, pinning her to the wall. He wanted to make her come as many times as he could before he got inside her, because once he was, he knew he wouldn't last long. Not this first time.

He took her lips again and massaged those pretty breasts with both hands, moving against her until she was whimpering and grinding against him. Without warning, she arched, coming hard, moaning into his mouth as she rode it out. And he didn't even get her clothes off yet, he thought with raw hunger, wanting more.

He pulled back, taking in her bemused expression, the surprised satisfaction he saw there making him swell harder.

He thought she might be shy, embarrassed, but she linked her arms around his neck and leaned in, nipping at his lower lip.

"More" was all she said as she looked him in the eye.

"Oh, honey," he choked out. "There's plenty more."

Swinging her up into his arms, he turned to take her back to the fireplace, planning to dim the lights and strip that sweater off in the warm glow of the flames, when he stopped, his gaze drawn out the window.

He stared, uncertain what had caught his eye, but a bad feeling overcame him and he let Abby slide to her feet. He walked closer to the window that looked out over the field.

"Reece? What is it?"

Sirens screamed in the distance, and the glow in the air over the field that had attracted his attention was not a figment of his imagination.

Her winery was on fire.

3

ABBY RESTED HER HEAD against Buttercup's soft neck and just thanked the heavens that the barns hadn't caught fire, too. That was something she couldn't even bear to think about.

Her house was badly damaged, unlivable after water from the hoses had ruined what fire had not, but the main rooms of the winery were reduced to cinders. The horse seemed to nuzzle her in comfort as she tried to hold her tears back, but couldn't, sobs racking her body.

What now?

The flickering light that she'd been trying to have fixed ended up being wires that the fire investigator said were probably chewed through by a mouse or squirrel in the wall. When the tree lights had been plugged in, she hadn't thought twice about it, but the circuit had been overloaded and started the fire. It had spread inside the walls before consuming the entire winery.

If she'd been home, she might have been killed if she had been sleeping or overcome with smoke, although she had detectors everywhere. On the other hand, if she had been there, she might have been able to call the fire department sooner, and maybe it wouldn't have been so bad, such a complete loss.

Instead, she'd been at Reece's, in his arms, ready to say yes to anything he asked, while her family's legacy burned to the ground.

She had to get away from the swarm of people. The firemen were still keeping watch, even though the fire was officially out, the insurance and other investigators were there, along with some neighbors, friends…and Reece. Everyone wanted to help, but she'd insisted on being alone for just a few minutes.

She needed the peace to think about what she would say to her parents, how she could tell them what happened.

Guilt assailed her. How could she explain why she hadn't been there? That she'd been so busy, and so distracted by thoughts of Reece, that she hadn't thought twice about the tree lights or the electrical problem?

She groaned, standing straight, wiping the tears away. No time for this now.

She had to get the insurance settled and cancel the wedding they'd been planning—that would be another tough phone call. The couple wouldn't likely find another venue with only weeks until the wedding, but there wasn't anything she could do about that. Abby would have to refund their deposits. That was going to hurt.

She'd see if Hannah would let her move in for a while, though it would mean driving back and forth to Ithaca daily, or maybe her insurance would pick up a room at the local inn, for a while at least.

"I thought you might be down here," a familiar voice said behind her.

"Hannah," she said, trying to sound normal, but her voice cracked under the weight of her exhaustion, being up all night, dealing with it all.

Hannah was across the barn, holding her arms out and Abby didn't hesitate.

She held on to her friend, just for a minute, but it was Reece's arms she knew she'd been seeking. Remembering how good it had been, not just the sexual part, but the way he'd held her against his hard chest later, when they'd watched the firemen work, had kept her from losing it altogether. She wanted that comfort back.

No, no, no. That was how she'd gotten into this mess, sort of.

"You okay?" Hannah asked, stepping back and smiling as two of the barn cats wound their way around her ankles.

"Yeah. I'm just so thankful the barns are far away from the house," she said, stroking Beau's silky nose. All of the animals were okay.

"That is a good thing," Hannah agreed, chuckling softly as Buttercup snorted happily in response to more scratching. "Everything else can be replaced. It was a straightforward electrical fire. The insurance agent is already on it. Things can be rebuilt."

"True, but I don't know if that will be enough," Abby said, too discouraged to be optimistic. "They can't start rebuilding until after winter, which means we're not only losing the Christmas events, but the spring wedding season and tastings as well. We lost almost all of the Riesling casks. With Reece selling, this could just be a killer blow," Abby said tightly, her throat constricting at the thought.

"How am I going to tell Mom and Dad? I feel so much like I've let them down," Abby said, sucking in more tears.

Hannah knew just what to do to drive the tears away.

"Speaking of Reece…he seemed awfully involved in helping you last night. And I couldn't help but notice when we went inside that at first his shirt wasn't buttoned up quite right. You know, like it had been put back together in a rush," she said, with mischief in her tone that made Abby's tears completely evaporate.

Abby groaned. Did everyone know where she'd been and what she was doing?

As if reading her mind, Hannah added, "He said he saw the fire from his house, got dressed and rushed down to help. Don't worry—he didn't give anything away, though I sure hope you're going to share details with your very best friend in the whole wide world, right? You know, about why Reece was really getting dressed?"

Unbelievably, Abby had to laugh. Leave it to Hannah, even in the middle of utter loss. When all Abby had left was this barn and what was in it, her friend found a way to lighten the mood.

Reece had been wonderful. He hadn't left her side until Hannah had arrived. He jumped in, talking to the firemen, police and the other people milling around, even opening up the main room of his winery for people to come in, get warm and have coffee. At some moment when she'd been talking to the fire investigator, Abby had lost track of him and assumed he had gone back home.

"Thanks, I needed that," she said, taking a breath and feeling a bit better. "And there aren't many details to share. Not really. I went down to Reece's, brought some wine, hoping to talk…one thing lead to another, but before it went too far, he noticed the fire. That was pretty much it," she said, shrugging.

"Oh, I doubt that's it. The man's interested—he couldn't take his eyes off you, especially when that hunky fireman was talking to you, and standing a little too close, by the way," Hannah said.

"You're imagining things. Reece was just helping out. We're old friends and we shared a moment—instigated by a bottle of wine. It's best forgotten. I have enough to worry about now." Abby's attention snapped to the barn doors, where outside, she heard a woman's voice, and then sharp, shrieking words. She couldn't make out what was being said, but several colorful curses punctuated the diatribe.

Abby headed out of the barn to find Sandra Towers, the Christmas bride-to-be, standing in the middle of the yard in front of the blackened mess of Abby's winery, wild-eyed and in tears. She spotted Abby then and marched across the lawn, obviously ready for a confrontation.

Great, just what she needed right now. Abby sighed. She shouldn't bothered with having quiet time in the barn. She should have been on the phone doing damage control.

Too late, she admitted, as Sandra met her, almost standing nose-to-nose, and Abby backed up slightly.

"Sandra, I am so sorry. I was about to make phone calls—"

"I saw this on the news and couldn't believe it. I had to see for myself. This is a nightmare! How could you let this happen?" the prospective bride yelled, clearly not thinking straight.

Abby tried to be patient. This was hard on everyone, and brides were under a lot of stress in general. Sandra wasn't finished, obviously.

"What am I going to do? The invitations are all sent! Everything is scheduled! How are you going to fix this?" she demanded, and Abby pulled in a deep breath, closing her eyes, reaching for patience.

"Sandra, I know it's terrible, and I wish there was better news, but I'll definitely refund all of your down payment and try to help you find another—"

"The wedding is twenty-five days away! There is *no* other place," the young woman wailed. "I know, I checked them all. We have family coming in from Europe! You had better fix this or...or...we'll *sue!*"

Abby was quite sure the normally pleasant woman was just distraught, and also was sure—mostly—that she had no basis for a lawsuit whatsoever. Still, it was hard to remain calm, and she was digging her nails into her palms in her effort to do so.

Suddenly, Reece appeared, putting his large hand on her shoulder. She looked up in surprise, noting the circles under his eyes. He was obviously exhausted, too.

"Abby, could I talk to you for a minute?" he said politely. "Excuse us for just a moment," he said to Sandra with a smile. Amazingly, the young woman didn't pitch yet another fit.

Abby walked with him to a spot about twenty feet away and wondered how she could still feel his touch when she was wearing her coat and he had put on a pair of heavy gloves. Maybe the same way she'd had a scream-worthy orgasm against his thigh—apparently clothes were not a barrier to sex with Reece Winston.

"First things first," he said, dragging her away from her thoughts and producing a steaming travel cup to her. She could smell the aroma of the hot coffee inside. She took the cup, took a sip and peered at him over the top, thanking him with a look of bliss.

"I came out to bring you that and heard the shouting. I guess you had a wedding planned soon?"

She groaned and nodded. "Two days before Christmas."

"And that is the blushing bride," he stated more than asked.

"Yes." Abby sighed. "I don't blame her for being upset, but I didn't expect her to come out here and go nuts.… Still, I can imagine it's a mess for her, too."

Reece nodded. "She's obviously missing the point that you lost a lot more than she did last night," he said in a hard tone, peering over to where Sandra stood, arms crossed, watching them.

Abby didn't say anything, but took another sip of the strong coffee so the heat would scorch away the tightening in her throat. He was sticking up for her again, just like he did when the mean boy had picked on her about her braces.

"Thanks, but I have to find some way to compensate

her. Now is as good a time as any. Then I have to find out what our exact losses are and call my parents. That is going to be so awful…" she said, and didn't dare meet his eyes, lest his sympathy weaken her resolve not to cry again.

Normally Abby never cried, not even during sappy movies, but she was overwrought and exhausted. Right now, she needed to concentrate on business.

"I have an idea," Reece said.

"If we try to lock her in the barn, I don't think anyone will believe that she's a runaway bride," Abby tried to joke, but it fell flat.

Reece smiled slightly. He tipped her chin up with his fingers, making her meet his eyes, which were sympathetic, but not in a bad way. In a silvery, soft way that made her remember his kiss.

"What?" she asked, almost panicked that amid everything, she could still lust for Reece.

"Use Winston wineries for the wedding, and for any other events you have this month. You can move your wines down to our room, and we'll feature both vineyards, if you don't mind—yours and ours. I need to clear out inventory before we sell, so it could work out for all of us."

Abby stared. Had he just offered for her to use his winery?

"But…you're selling," she said blankly. What if the place sold quickly? She'd only become reaquainted with Reece two days ago—could she trust him? She couldn't make promises that she'd break again later on.

"Don't worry about that. I can work it out so that whoever buys us, they don't close until after the wedding, at least. If it takes longer, we can figure it out as we go, but in the meanwhile, you're welcome to run your business out of our front rooms."

Abby was stunned and unsure what to say, but she couldn't think of one good reason to say no, except what had happened between them the night before. What had *almost* happened. If she and Reece were going into business together, even temporarily, she couldn't let that happen again.

"I don't know what to say…it's so generous of you," she admitted. "It would save me so much, not having to refund the deposit on this wedding. And all you want me to do is sell your wines, too?"

That wouldn't be hard; the Winstons made spectacular wines, and she had lost several barrels in the fire, so this could be the perfect solution.

As long as they could keep their hands—and wonderful, muscular thighs—to themselves, she thought silently.

"I thought you said your Realtor wanted you keeping the property empty, neutral? I'd have to decorate, and there would be people around all the time…."

Reece didn't look concerned. "I know. I'm sure he can work around it. The place is just sitting there. I already sent the staff home and was going to run the main room myself for a few weeks, but you obviously could use it."

Her heart lightened as she considered, and she felt hopeful for the first time all morning. This could save her, in more ways than one.

"We'd have to, um, keep things strictly business, though," she said, hoping he got her drift.

This would also give her the perfect opportunity to talk with Reece about selling. Maybe she could convince him there was a better way…and give her time to figure out what that was.

"Whatever you want, Abby. I'm just a friend, trying to help. No strings attached," he said, though she could tell from the heat in his eyes that he was remembering the night before, too.

Could *she* keep things "strictly business" with Reece?

"I guess I could ask Sandra," she said, though she couldn't imagine it wouldn't be an acceptable option. Winston wineries was far fancier than Abby's reception room, and with the same beautiful views.

"I could try booking rooms for the wedding party at Tandy's Inn, and I'll need one, too," she added, thinking out loud.

"We have some rooms upstairs. Mom used them more for guests, but they would work for your wedding party to dress or spend the night. You should stay at the house. You're more than welcome."

"I don't think that's a good idea," she said. "I mean, I don't want to intrude. You're being kind enough as it is."

He looked at her as if she was talking nonsense. "It's a big house, Abby, and you'd be near your barns and the winery. There's no reason to pay for a room when we have six empty ones upstairs in the house."

Abby chewed her lip, feeling like she was jumping into the frying pan after the fire, but her house wouldn't be habitable for quite some time. Staying at Tandy's, even though it was right there in the village, wouldn't be as convenient as being at Reece's.

Or as tempting.

Steeling her resolve, she nodded. *Put on your big girl panties and do this, Abby,* she mentally nudged herself. *Just be sure you keep them on.*

Ha. Like panties would matter.

"What?" he said.

She coughed, realizing she might have said that under her breath.

"Uh, nothing." She looked up at Reece. Surely last night was a fluke, the result of wine and reminiscing. They could do this. "Thank you, Reece. You have no idea what this means to me."

"It's my pleasure, Abby. Just let me know anything you need," he said.

His pleasure? Anything she needed? Ohmygod, this was a bad idea.

With another squeeze to her arm before he turned away, he walked back toward his house. Where she would be sleeping tonight.

But not with him.

Abby groaned as she went to talk to Sandra. Hannah was absolutely going to love this.

REECE STOPPED AND looked back, watched Abby walk away, her stride lighter than before. That made him feel better, too, that there was something he could do to help.

She chatted with the young woman whom he had heard yelling at the top of her spoiled, self-interested lungs when he had arrived with coffee. The two women chatted a few seconds, and the bride threw her arms around Abby. Apparently his solution worked for her.

He nodded in satisfaction, strolling the rest of the way to his place. This path over the field would get a lot of wear back and forth over the next month, he thought.

Surprisingly, suddenly, he was looking forward to Abby's company in the big house. Normally being alone didn't bother him. In fact, he preferred it, but this could work.

He hoped.

He might be losing his mind, actually, but what was done was done. It hadn't even occurred to him until he'd heard the woman yelling about suing Abby, and he'd taken in the exhaustion that bruised the pale skin under her eyes and the strain that pinched at her as she tried to maintain her composure.

How could he not offer her the use of the winery? It's what any decent neighbor, and old family friend, would do.

Right?

Right. It really wasn't an excuse to spend more time with Abby while he was here, or to hopefully have her in his bed, even though she warned him they wouldn't be mixing business with pleasure.

He hoped to change her mind on that score. Soon.

He'd have to call Charles, who wasn't going to be happy, not at all, but Reece knew his parents would agree—this was the neighborly thing to do.

Especially when his neighbor was as sexy as Abby, with lips like satin and a body that moved against his like she was made for him.

As much as he meant his promise of a no-strings arrangement, he knew she wanted him, too. He could feel it every time he touched her.

And he planned to touch her. A lot.

His cell phone started ringing as soon as he got through the door, and he saw it was his brother, Ben. Immediately concerned that something was wrong with his father, fantasies about Abby disintegrated and Reece answered the call, tense.

"Ben, what's wrong?"

"Whoa, brother, calm down. Everything's fine—but you sound upset. What's going on?" he asked sharply.

Ben had fallen in love with the game of golf when he was a kid, though he was never more than an average player. But he never gave up on his dream of being involved in the sport, and landed a graduate degree in landscape architecture, with a specialization in designing golf courses. He's spent years working with some of the best designers, building his name, and finally accumulated the backing to open his own course, his own design. Then he met his wife, Kelly, and they had two beautiful kids now. Ben had a stable, solid life.

Reece, unlike Ben, had lived a more precarious, adventure-driven existence. He'd finished college, but the business admin degree was something he'd pursued because he didn't really know what else he was going to do with his life. Reece had always bragged that he liked not knowing what was around the next corner. He never stopped moving, until recently.

"Sorry. I guess I just assumed something was wrong with Dad," Reece said.

When had his love of adventure turned into him expecting a disaster every time the phone rang? Was this part of the post-traumatic stress disorder that his neurologist had warned about—and that Reece had dismissed—that was often the result of serious car crashes?

"He's fine. Mom, too. But they're worried about you, up there, alone, especially for the holidays. I offered to come up. I can book a flight today if you want some help getting things done there, arranging the sale, the move, whatever. We could have some serious brother time," Ben said. "Go ice fishing or something."

Reece smiled. "That would be great, but I don't want to take you away from Kelly and the kids so close to the holidays. I'm good, and in fact, things have taken an interesting turn," he said, going on to explain about the fire and offering use of the winery to Abby.

Ben whistled. "Wow. Never boring for you, is it?"

Reece laughed. "Yeah, you could say that. Could you fill in Mom and Dad? I assumed they wouldn't mind."

"I'm sure they'll be fine with it. More than fine even," Ben said and Reece closed his eyes, hearing the grin in his brother's voice.

"Don't start, Ben, and don't make them think this is anything other than what it is."

"They'd just love for you to move back, whether it's to run the winery or not. And I saw Abby when we were there for Christmas last year. She filled out nice, huh?"

Reece's hackles raised, hearing his brother's frankly admiring tone. But he wasn't surprised. A man would have to be gay or dead not to notice Abby.

"Yeah, but it's not like that."

Yes, it was.

"Really? I know you, Reece. And I know you've had a thing for her ever since you were about six years old."

"How could you know that? You were only four," Reece said with a scoff.

"Yeah, well, I remember all the years after that, too. I never could figure out why you just didn't ask her out. Hell, I almost did, just to make you jealous," Ben said, laughing at his brother's expense.

And it might have worked, Reece acknowledged. But that was then. They were only kids.

And he wasn't Ben. Reece didn't do permanent with anything, not when the real love of his life was getting behind the wheel of a car and driving two hundred miles an hour for a living. He'd seen too many racers leave families behind, after they had sacrificed everything to the sport, including their lives.

"Ben, seriously, please make sure it's okay with them. I'm still planning to sell and to move back to France. I want to race again. It's all I want."

Except for Abby.

He shook his head of the thought. Sure, he *wanted* her—in his bed—but his life was still on the track, on the other side of the Atlantic.

Ben's disappointment was carefully veiled behind a general remark, but he agreed to what Reece asked. After some more discussion about the winery and its future, Reece put the phone back on the mahogany table by the window. Right there, the night before, he'd pressed Abby up against the wall with every intention of making her his.

For the night.

He still planned to do that—for a week, or a month— and he'd make sure she knew that up front, too. She'd use Winston to get through the holiday and the wedding, and they'd share some good times to make up for what they missed back in high school—or not, if Abby stuck to her guns about business only—then they would both go on with their lives. It was that simple.

Reece ignored the mocking laugh in his head as he went upstairs to get a room set up for Abby.

4

Two DAYS LATER, Abby drove up the lake road, returning from a day of shopping. The sun hung low on the horizon, and she figured she had about an hour of dusky daylight left. Even with the shorter days, the snow helped keep things brighter longer. She turned into her driveway out of habit, forgetting that she meant to go to Reece's and unload her goods, but since she was here, figured she could check in on the horses. When she spotted the barn doors open, she froze.

Though they weren't susceptible to much crime, and though she was just across the field, she'd been worried about her horses. She'd barely had time to take care of Beau and Buttercup, having had to break her promise of a long ride and settle for leaving them out in the pasture.

But that door shouldn't be open. She knew for a fact that she'd locked it when she left that morning.

The stale scent of smoke from the fire still clung faintly to the crisp winter air as she hopped out of the car and made her way down to the barn. Slowly opening the door, she peered inside and saw no one but Shadow, their black lab, who came bounding to greet her, and Buttercup. But no Beau. The door to his stall was wide open, though it appeared undamaged.

Abby's heart fell to her feet and she stepped inside, instantly noting that Beau's tack was gone as well.

Frowning, she pulled out her cell phone.

"Hannah? Are you riding Beau?" she asked as soon as her friend picked up, though usually Hannah would let Abby know if she was coming by. Also, Hannah typically rode Buttercup, who was somewhat smaller.

"Uh, no, why would you ask?"

Abby put a hand to her forehead, closing her eyes to stave off panic, and walked back out the door to breathe in the cold air and calm down.

"Beau's not here, neither is his tack, and I've been gone all day—"

She stopped midsentence as she caught sight of a figure getting closer, down by the edge of the field. Hannah was upset, too, and told her to hang up and call the police, but a few moments later, Abby saw with a wash of relief that that wouldn't be necessary.

"It's Reece. Reece has him," she said into the phone, and then hung up as the rider and the horse came closer.

Abby had never seen Reece on horseback. She didn't even know he could ride. His family always had dogs, but never horses.

"Reece!" she called, waving, and he waved back, heading toward her.

He looked like every cowboy fantasy she'd ever had, sitting tall on Beau, his camel-colored coat and hat contrasting with the steed's dark chestnut coloring as they approached her. Beau whinnied in welcome, and Abby was so relieved he was okay she realized she was shaking.

"Hey, are you all right? What's wrong?" Reece asked as he came up next to her.

"I—I saw the door open and Beau gone… I didn't know where he was. I thought maybe someone stole him. The police told me to be careful about people poking around here, which I guess some people do when they find out about burned buildings…." She trailed off, petting the horse's soft cheek with a sigh of relief.

"Ah, damn, Abby. Sorry about that. You left the barn keys on the counter, and I was feeling antsy. I knew you hadn't had any time to get them out for a ride, so I figured I'd do it for you," he said, clearly apologetic.

"That's so good of you, Reece. I guess I didn't think of you because I didn't even know you rode," she admitted.

"I learned in France. Haven't had the chance to ride in a while, but it felt good."

"Did you ride both of them?"

"No, I figured I'd give them both a short turn around the field, so I was just coming back for Buttercup."

Abby nodded. "Let me grab a saddle and I'll join you, if you don't mind. They can have a longer ride that way, and I could use some fresh air, too."

"Sure, that would be great," he agreed, and a little while later Abby was on Buttercup, riding alongside Reece on the lake path, more relaxed than she had been in days.

"I needed this. I'm glad you had the idea to take them

out," she said. "I feel so guilty when I can't tend to them like I always did, but it seems like the winery takes over my life sometimes."

"I hear you. I thought I would like to get some pets at home in France, but I don't want to kennel them or pay pet-sitters when I'm away, which is usually a lot."

The easy companionship between them seemed enhanced by the quiet of the trail and the rhythmic gait of the horses.

"You have a house there?" she asked.

"Yes, outside of the Talence, near the Bordeaux region. There's a lot of industry there, as well as wine and some universities. I found a house outside of the town that allowed me to go into the city if I wanted to, but to retreat when I needed to, as well. It's an older house, and I have been fixing it up slowly, when I have the opportunity."

"Bordeaux? So you left wine country to live in wine country?" she said with a soft laugh, so he knew she wasn't criticizing.

"I guess so. I did intend to study wines when I went there, and then I discovered racing."

"Funny how you had to go that far to find it, when we've lived with the Glen under our noses all our lives."

"I know. But we never really went to the races when we were kids. Ben and Dad spent more time playing golf, which I never took to. I went to a few races at the Glen, but at that point in time I was more interested in making out with whatever girl I met there instead of watching the race," he said with a self-effacing grin.

She laughed. "That's changed?"

"Mostly. I rarely date in season. I can't afford the distraction, not that there aren't plenty of offers."

"You're modest, too," she teased.

"Hey, it's true. Groupies follow racing just like any sport, and some of the guys take advantage, but it's never been my thing."

"So you don't date?"

"Not in season, not really," he said, and she considered that, leaving the subject alone for a while. She hadn't intended to turn her questions into a fishing expedition about his love life.

So he wasn't saying he didn't see women, he just didn't see them while he was driving. She guessed that made sense. She never assumed he was a saint.

"How about you?" he asked.

"What?"

"You date much?"

"Now and then, nothing serious. I've been so busy with the business since Mom and Dad left. It takes up all of my time, really."

"Lucky for me," he said, almost under his breath, and Abby blinked and shot him a look, unsure she had actually heard that. She decided not to ask for clarification, and they stopped talking for a while, making their way back up the far end of the trail, and across the fields to the barns.

"I'll get the door," she said, dismounting easily and making her way over to pull the doors open.

It was darker by the time they returned, and in the soft, golden light that spilled out of the barn, he looked even more handsome, she thought. He smiled, but there was something tight about it. He didn't dismount, and Abby wondered what the problem was.

"Are you okay?" she asked, unsure what to make of his sudden silence. Beau shifted and snorted, dancing under Reece, eager to be brushed and fed now that he'd worked off some energy.

"Yeah, I'm fine," Reece almost growled between clenched teeth, and in the next second, he swung his leg over to the ground. Abby was horrified to see that as he landed, his leg gave way and his other foot never quite made it out of the stirrup, making Beau jump sideways nervously.

"Reece, oh, no," she breathed, steadying Beau and making her way over to help him up so that he could get his foot out of the stirrup to regain his balance.

"Are you okay?" she said, looking down and stepping carefully. There was no ice.

Reece was on his feet now, his expression reflecting stifled pain, and he walked forward, taking Beau's reins as he limped into the barn without a word.

Abby frowned, following. "Reece? Are you okay?"

He paused, his posture stiff. "I'm fine, Abby. My leg just fell asleep."

"Oh. I thought it might be the injury from your accident," she said, knowing that now she *was* fishing. He knew it, too.

He rested his forehead on his hand, where it lay on Beau's back, as if he was looking for patience, or a way to escape.

Finally, he straightened and looked at her again. "It

is. It's not serious. I kept my leg in the same position for too long and it went numb. No big deal."

"It could have been a big deal if you couldn't get back up or if Beau had taken off in a panic or trampled you," she said. "Does this happen often?"

"I don't need the third degree, Abby. I just should have been more careful dismounting. Can we leave it? Okay?"

"I'm concerned," she said, refusing to feel guilty. If that had happened when he was alone, he could have been badly hurt.

"I know," he said, sounding tired. "But it's fine."

She didn't think so, but she bit back any more comments. The easy mood they'd had all evening was now replaced with tension, and she nodded, grabbing a brush and getting Buttercup set for the night.

Reece didn't say anything more, and he was still limping, if a little less severely, as he put Beau away and left, walking back to the house without another word. She would have offered to drive him, since she had to take her car back anyway, but somehow she didn't think that would help.

Obviously falling from the horse hadn't only reminded him of his injuries, it had probably dented his ego to fall in front of her. Silly, but she knew men were like that sometimes.

"I guess I stepped in it," she said to Buttercup, petting the mare's sleek coat. The horses looked at her with calm patience, and Beau snorted again.

Abby smirked at him. "Oh, sure, take his side," she said affectionately to the animal, locking the barn and making her way back to the house, as well.

THE FOLLOWING AFTERNOON, ABBY had done little more than run back and forth to Ithaca and Syracuse, dealing with insurance issues and setting up contractors. Today, she'd caught up on more personal needs, purchasing a stash of clothing to replace some basics that were ruined in the fire, taking what she could salvage to the cleaners and loading up some food for Reece's kitchen.

He hadn't really stocked the kitchen, probably because he didn't think he'd be there long, and he would probably eat out, she figured. But Abby liked to cook and she liked to eat, so food was a necessity. She also needed supplies for tastings—crackers, chocolates and cheeses. She wanted to make up for her snafu the evening before, when Reece fell. She couldn't blame him for being embarrassed, and she had been too nosy.

She planned to make him a nice dinner—it was the least she could do, given his generosity. Visiting markets in the city to find the ingredients she needed had been the first fun she'd had in days.

She'd also taken time to walk around a bit, enjoying the atmosphere and having a moment to herself. Ithaca was such a lovely little city, a neat combination of funky college town with an active arts community and working-class neighborhoods.

Set at the southern edge of Cayuga Lake, Ithaca hosted two colleges, including the famous Cornell University, her alma mater. The city also had more eateries per capita than New York City. It was surrounded by beautiful hillsides, vineyards, gorges and waterfalls, and the town had a wonderful underground mall by the Commons, the famous Moosewood restaurant and the farmer's market, where she shopped every week. She loved what every season had to offer, and the place was as woven into who she was as much as anything else in her life.

How could Reece have wanted to leave so badly? She had everything she needed here, and though everyone enjoyed a vacation away, Abby always liked coming home.

Her worries about staying at his home had been groundless—she'd been gone so much, usually working, and apparently he was busy doing things, too, so they'd barely seen each other long enough to say good morning since the horse-riding incident.

She had to walk past his room, trying not to notice the light on under the door, and continue down the hall to a large guest bedroom that looked out over the lake. The guest room was twice the size of her own bedroom in her house, and she loved the view of the lake, facing the opposite direction of her burnt buildings. She appreciated Reece being so thoughtful as to spare her the reminder.

Still, even with the beautiful view and the big bed, she hadn't slept great since the fire. It was hard to not think about everything looming over her, and she hadn't been able to contact her parents yet, which was weighing on her. Then there was the itching desire for Reece, the need to touch him, to be close to him, that she couldn't quite stop fantasizing about.

She finally finished putting everything away and left out only what she needed for dinner—a lovely pork roast, vegetables and potatoes, the perfect comfort meal for a winter evening.

She planned to make some appetizers as well, and of course, open some wine.

She paused as she started the roast—would Reece take this the wrong way? She merely wanted to do her part, to thank him for his help and to feel at home as much as she could. As much as she was tempted to give in to her fantasies, doing so would only make everything so much more complicated, and right now the last thing she needed was more complication in her life.

On second thought, maybe she shouldn't open any wine.

The phone on the wall next to her rang, and without thinking she picked it up.

"Hello?"

"Um, hello?" a heavily accented woman's voice responded, obviously confused. "I am looking for Reece?"

"He's not home. May I take a message?" Abby asked, reaching for a pen.

A heavy sigh met her request. "And who is this?" the woman asked, her "this" sounding more like "theese."

None of your bees-niss, Abby felt like saying, feeling annoyed. "I'm a friend of Reece's. May I take a message?"

"A friend, eh? You may tell him Danielle called," she said, a bit huffily, Abby thought. Maybe it was the accent.

"Danielle…last name?"

"He will know," she said with an aggravatingly sexy laugh.

"Sure."

"Be sure he receives the message, please."

"Of course," Abby said. "Goodbye."

She set the phone down, wondering why she felt so peevish. It was obviously just a friend of Reece's from Europe calling. Abby sighed, shaking it off.

She bet that Reece had *lots* of friends with sexy accents back in France. Plopping the roast into the Dutch oven a little more forcefully than she planned, she splashed stock on her shirt and shook her head.

Ridiculous to be this put out by the idea of Reece with other women. Sexier, more sophisticated, French women.

Well, she couldn't compete and didn't want to, she decided, tying on an apron to avoid further damage. Putting the woman and her snooty accent out of her mind, she turned on the radio and focused on cutting vegetables and making her appetizers.

She quickly worked her way out of her snit and was shimmying across the kitchen, singing at the top of her lungs to Mariah Carey's version of "All I Want For Christmas Is You." She was on her way to put the tray of cheese and fruit in the refrigerator, but nearly dropped it all when she met Reece's amused expression as he stood, propped in the doorway, grinning from ear to ear.

"Reece!" she said, fumbling and blushing to the roots of her hair. "How long have you been standing there?"

He pursed his lips thoughtfully. "Mmm…about from the first chorus," he said lightly, still smiling.

"Oh, God," she said, covering her face, shaking with embarrassed laughter.

"I have to admit, the apron adds a certain panache to your performance," he teased.

She looked down at the sexy apron she wore, a

Cheetah print with red ruffles and a bow at the neck-line. Hannah had bought it for her birthday as a funny gift, and it had never been worn, especially since an embroidered patch on the pocket read Hot Stuff.

As if this wasn't embarrassing enough.

It was one of the few items from the kitchen pantry that didn't get ruined. She hadn't thought twice when she'd donned it, unused to an audience while cooking.

"It was a gag gift," she explained. "From Hannah."

Reece scanned her up and down appreciatively and walked over to where she stood.

"What smells so good?"

"I thought I would make us dinner, as a thank-you… and also because I like to cook. It destressed me," she said, trying to keep her voice level as he ran a finger over the edge of the bow, the tip of his finger brushing against her skin at the edge of her shirt.

"That's nice of you. I haven't had a home-cooked dinner in a while," he said sincerely, but there was a glint in his eye.

"This is every man's fantasy, you know," he said, tugging at the bow to pull her forward against him. "A sexy woman in the kitchen making him dinner after a long day."

She rolled her eyes. "Puh-leese. I can't imagine you ever having a fantasy that mundane," she said, and then shook her head.

Why was she still standing here, so close to him?

He lowered his head and nibbled at her earlobe, making her yelp.

"Reece! What are you doing?"

He chuckled against her skin. "Just having a taste,"

he said, nibbling again. "I think you splashed something on your neck. Let me get it," he offered.

It was news to her that the nerves in her earlobes were connected directly to her knees, which seemed to turn to water. She planted her hands against his chest and tried to push. The man was rock-solid.

"I have appetizers," she said breathlessly.

"Not what I'm hungry for," he said against her neck, nipping at her speeding pulse.

"Reece," she said as calmly as she could. "We agreed we had to keep things only business."

"You said that, but I only agreed out of politeness," he whispered, his breath against her lips. "I said I'd do whatever you want," he added, brushing a thumb over a very hard nipple, making her gasp, his eyes meeting hers. "You want?"

Oh, did she ever.

"It's not a good idea," she said lamely, still unable to force her feet to move. He just felt too damned good.

"Abby," he said, laughing softly, "it's just me."

That was like saying, "It's just dynamite," to her mind.

He proceeded to cover her lips with light, soft, teasing kisses that made her grab on to him, curling her fingers into his jacket as she sought more. He didn't accommodate her until she groaned and worked her hands up to his neck, holding him still as she kissed him, taking what she needed.

She was weak, but she just couldn't work up the energy to care.

"I guess you're not angry at me anymore for the other night?" she asked, breathless.

His brow wrinkled, as if he was surprised. "I never was angry with you. Just frustrated, and a little embarassed. I'm sorry if I let you think otherwise," he said. "Let me apologize properly."

Reece walked her backward as they kissed hungrily, lifting her almost without her noticing until she sat on the kitchen counter. He settled in between her thighs, deepening the kiss until breathing was unheard of and—as far as Abby was concerned—completely unnecessary.

"Nothing mundane about this fantasy from where I'm standing," he said when he broke the kiss, her face framed in his hands, his eyes devouring her.

He'd tugged the tie of the apron loose and continued to trail kisses down her throat. Slowly his hand moved down to cover her breast before pushing up the edge of her blouse, and Abby was beyond arguing. She wanted the frustrating barrier of their clothes gone and to know his touch on her bare skin.

The sheer idea made her dizzy.

He had her shirt off in a split second. She reached behind to unclasp her bra, his hands covering her, spilling over with the fullness of her bare breasts.

"Damn, babe, where were you hiding these in high school?" he said appreciatively, bending to nuzzle her intimately, her hand slipping into his hair to press him close. She wanted his mouth on her in the worst way.

"I've lost a little weight since then," she said with a chuckle, "and I guess I filled out in other areas. Late bloomer," she finished on a sigh. He'd taken her aching nipple into his mouth, sucking hard, then laving with his tongue until she was writhing on the counter.

"You're so sweet," he said, working his lips over

her stomach and taking her hand, placing it to her own breast as he watched. His eyes darkened intensely as she touched herself, tweaking and pulling as he slowly unzipped her jeans while he watched and kissed.

She stopped, and put her hand on his.

"You first. You have far too many clothes on," she said provocatively.

He nodded and stepped back, not breaking the gaze between them as he took his jacket off and threw it on the island behind him, then made quick work of his sweater.

She gasped.

He was gorgeous. Lean and muscled, his tanned skin proved he'd spent the majority of his winters in sunnier places, and she loved how his shoulders and biceps flexed as he tore the garment off.

Then she realized he'd stilled, looking at her strangely, more tensely.

"I'm sorry. I didn't think to warn you," he said, glancing down, and only then did she even notice some of the scars, remnants of a burn by his shoulder, and what looked like thin lines from surgery a little lower.

"That wasn't what I was staring at," she said, wanting nothing more than to touch him, thinking only of that. "But it doesn't bother me at all. Come here," she commanded softly.

He walked over to her and pushed his hands into her hair, pulling her up hard against him. Her breasts crushed delightfully against his hard skin, his mouth plundering hers.

She managed to retain enough focus to move her

hands to the front of his jeans, undoing the buttons, and sliding her hand down inside.

Now it was his turn to gasp, breaking the kiss. He leaned his forehead on her shoulder as he trembled beneath her touch. He was hard, thick and hot in her hand. She stroked him, loving the friction of his skin against hers.

His breathing was labored as he ground out, "No, stop." His teasing tone gone.

She froze. Had she hurt him? Done something wrong?

"What?" she asked

"I'll come," he said tensely. "It's been months, since before the accident, and this feels too good," he explained, pushing away a stray hair that had landed in her eyes.

Abby couldn't think of a single thing he could have said that would have turned her on more.

She smiled, feeling feminine, powerful.

"Seems like you're well overdue then," she said, closing in for a kiss. She continued stroking him, rubbing her thumb over the slippery head of his cock and mimicking the rubbing motion with her tongue against his.

In mere seconds he exploded, thrusting into her hand, groaning deeply into her mouth as he came. When he broke the kiss, his beautiful chest heaved with hard breaths, his cheeks flushed and his eyes were still hot as he looked at her.

"I don't think anything in my life will ever feel better than that did," he said, still catching his breath.

She smiled again. "Maybe we should go upstairs and find out."

She was more than ready to take him to bed, and she didn't want to wait. To hell with complications. Complications could feel damned good, from where she was sitting.

"What about dinner?"

"That roast has a couple hours yet. It can just simmer," she said, the last word coming out more sexually than she intended.

She would take the memory of the way he looked at her—a gaze rich with lust, gratitude and anticipation—to her grave.

The loud sound of an engine and the hissing of air brakes made her jump, and they stared at each other in confusion before she looked at the clock and realized.

"You're expecting someone?" Reece asked.

"Yes! I completely forgot—it's the trees," she said, scrambling to get her bra on and trying to find her blouse before the nursery delivery guy came to the door.

"Trees?"

"Christmas trees. I completely forgot he was bringing them today," she explained.

Reece looked bemused, but followed her lead and grabbed his shirt, buttoning up his jeans.

"You mean, tree, singular?"

"No, sixteen of them," she said, and washed her hands quickly, grabbing a coat from the hook where she had left it earlier.

"Sixteen?" he echoed.

She grinned, her lusty thoughts fading to the background. "Three for the tasting rooms, a dozen for the decorating contest and one for the house. C'mon, you can help me with them."

As they walked out into the crisp air where two men unloaded a flatbed truck loaded with trees, Abby couldn't help but feel that their arrival might just have saved her from herself. As much as she wanted Reece, and wanted to give in, it would make her life an even greater mess. Right now, that was something she didn't need. As they spent the next few hours setting up Christmas trees, she tried to convince herself she was okay with that.

5

REECE FROWNED AT THE jungle of boxes and bins that crowded the main room of his house. Even more so since there was a huge tree in the corner, by the two front windows, and then more bags of new ornaments Abby had purchased. He looked at the tree again. It had to be eight feet tall. It had taken two hours to get the trees off the truck and in place. Two hours when he could have been making love to Abby, but while he had been helping with setting up trees, she had been hauling out decorations, apparently having forgotten their moment in the kitchen.

Now he knew how much work it had been for his dad, who always brought the trees home and spent hours struggling to erect them, to get the "right side" showing—a tree quality that only his mother seemed able to assess.

"You really didn't have to get a tree for in here," he said, trying to be tactful. He would have skipped it, personally.

"It's your last Christmas in this house. There should

be a tree," she said, as if that was the most logical thing in the world.

Luckily, most of Abby's family ornaments and decorations had been salvageable, contained neatly in plastic bins in her basement where the water from the fire hoses hadn't damaged them.

He'd had to call his mother, but found several boxes of their own, including several that he remembered from childhood. After a fantastic dinner of succulent pork that was one of the best things he had eaten in a long time, they had opened up the boxes and pulled everything out, which created what appeared to be utter chaos to Reece's eyes.

But Abby apparently had that special, female, Christmas sense that told her what ornaments should go where, and why.

Did it really make a difference?

He could tell from the intense concentration on Abby's face and the way she bit her lip—which was sexy, as well as completely endearing—that if she had lost these bins in the fire, it would have been a terrible thing. They were clearly meaningful to her.

It wasn't that he disliked Christmas, but he'd managed to tactfully avoid it this year by staying here, alone, and now it looked like it had found him anyway. Normally he would spend most of his holiday—when he didn't come home—working, and just have dinner with friends on the day, call his family, relax. But it had been his idea to have Abby here, and so he sucked it up.

A few hours later, having strung all the lights, they were now picking through the decorations, deciding what should go where.

"The silver and white should go in the back room, for the wedding reception, and the grapes will go on the tree in the tasting room, of course," she said, pulling several boxes aside.

"Grapes? You have grape ornaments?"

"There's a little store down on the Commons, the one that sells Christmas stuff all year round—you know the one?" she said, looking at him askance.

"I don't think I was ever in there," he admitted. When he was a student, he spent more time partying than shopping, and in the years since, even when he came home, spent most of his time with his family and never went into town too much.

"Oh, they have the most unusual ornaments. All kinds of characters, food items, just…whatever. And every year we would go down to see if they had some different grape ornaments, or ones that maybe looked like tiny wine bottles—we have fewer of those. Eventually the owner just called us when he got new things in, and he would trade us ornaments for bottles of wine. We had enough to decorate one tree with them."

Reece smiled, enjoying her enthusiasm about such a simple thing. "It sounds great—I can't wait to see it."

"Well, we can do that one first then."

"Tonight?" he said, surprised.

"Yes—I don't know that we can get all four done, but I'd like to try. There aren't any tastings until Friday, thank God, but I have dozens of other things to do."

Reece hadn't been aware he was going to spend the entire evening decorating Christmas trees—he had planned on much more interesting activities, like getting Abby in his bed. But she seemed genuinely excited about the trees, and all things considered, he decided, why not?

"Okay, I'm in."

His agreement was worth the smile it elicited.

So, after all of the ornaments were separated, they hauled the boxes over to the tasting room, which in the case of Winston wineries, was completely separate from the house and a much more modern construction, with shining oak beams and plate glass windows around their sales area.

Large leather chairs were strewn around the actual tasting area, inviting guests to enjoy the view and the wine. There was a fireplace near the bar, behind which the bottles of wine were arranged. Hidden track lighting put a soft golden glow over the room, rather than anything harsh or too bright. There were double French doors at the back that led to a reception area and an outdoor deck that overlooked the lake.

"It's so pretty and spacious here. I feel like our little tasting room was about the size of your closet," Abby said with a laugh, setting down her box of ornaments with a sigh. "I hope I have enough business to justify you letting us use all this space. I'll need to run through a tour with you, too, if you don't mind, so that I can train Hannah and Carl, and we need to set up the wine displays still, and—"

Reece put both hands on her shoulders. "Abby. Stop. Right now, focus on the tree, just this tree. One thing. Tomorrow there will be time to think about the rest."

"I know, but there's so much—"

"I know there is. But we can't do it tonight, and anyway, it's been a while since I've decorated a tree, let alone four of them," he said with a grin. He leaned in to brush a kiss over her mouth when she seemed ready to argue again. "Let's enjoy it."

Taking a deep breath, her cheeks pink from the kiss—something he planned to repeat as often as possible—she nodded, smiling, too.

"Sorry. Once my mind gets rolling, I can't stop sometimes," she admitted.

"I know the feeling. I used to be like that before a race. The day before, the night before, I wouldn't be able to stop thinking of everything, double- and triple-checking every detail. But I had to learn to trust my team, and also, I needed to sleep. A tired driver isn't a good driver. By trying to do everything, I wasn't doing my job as well as I needed to."

"I know. It was easier before, when Mom and Dad were here, and Sarah, but then it seemed like it all just landed in my lap, and I got so used to thinking about it all, all the time." She cast a glance over her shoulder, back toward her burned winery, though she couldn't see it in the dark. "Now I don't know what to think."

"It will all work out," Reece said steadily. "Speaking of your mom and dad, have you talked to them yet?" He guessed that, depending on where her parents were exactly in earthquake-torn Haiti, communication could be a real challenge.

He was sorry he asked, as her face crumpled with distress. "No, I don't want to worry them with vague emails, so I certainly don't want to deliver the news to them that way. I have left messages, and I'm just waiting for them to call me back," she said, wringing her fingers together. "I'm dreading it. I hate that I let this happen. They'll be so upset," she said.

"I'm sure all that they'll care about is that you are okay. Everything else can be rebuilt. But it might be another sign you are overworked—you start trying to handle too many things, you miss important details, and that's when bad things happen."

"Like you were just saying, about racing. I know you don't like to talk about it," she said quickly, looking away as she pulled some ornaments from a box and turned toward the tree, motioning him to do the same. "But is that what happened with your accident? You were trying to do too much?"

He swallowed hard. In the middle of seducing Abby in the kitchen, Christmas tree chaos and having their wonderful dinner, he realized he hadn't thought about his accident once in several hours, maybe for the first time in a long time. He hated bringing it back up again, but he supposed it was only fair to at least answer her question.

"No, not this time. This was just one of those crazy, unfortunate things…. I actually can't remember the crash."

"You have amnesia?" she said with some surprise.

He nodded shortly. "They say it's normal in traumatic situations, like car crashes, and I had pretty serious head injuries. You probably know I was in a coma for a while," he said.

She nodded, and as they put ornaments on the tree, it was easier to share the things he didn't normally talk with anyone about, except for his doctors.

"I watched the video footage for the first time a month

ago. I blew out a tire and the roads were wet, but I don't know why I lost control so completely, and I guess I might never know. I've had tires go before and controlled it. This time…" he said, trailing off, shaking his head. "I just don't know."

Her hand was on his arm then, squeezing in a way meant to comfort, but he felt his pulse jump. Any touch from Abby seemed to make that happen.

"My dad always says the only control we have in life is self-control. We can control how we react, what we do, and that's it. You were—" she paused, catching her slip "—*are* a fantastic driver. Even if you can't remember, I'm sure you did everything you could. Like you said, sometimes things just happen."

"Your dad always was a smart guy. How would you know what kind of driver I am?" he asked, hanging his last ornament on the tree.

"Uh, um, well…" She took her hand from his arm and reached into the box for more decorations. "It stands to reason, right? You're one of the major players. They said you could be the next Clark or Stewart."

His eyes widened. "You follow racing?"

She paused, leaning into the box, and he realized she'd let on more than she meant to. It warmed him in a whole different way that she had followed his career. He never would have guessed.

"I just caught things on the news. Hometown boy makes it big in Europe, you know, and you came back and drove at the Glen that one time," she said, gathering an armful of ornaments and returning to the tree.

"Did you come to that race?" he asked. It had only

been an exhibition run, a charity event, but he'd had no idea she was there.

"Some friends wanted to go, so I tagged along."

"I see."

"You see what?"

He shrugged, unable to resist the temptation to egg her on a little. "You followed my racing, you came to my exhibition…clearly you never quite got over your crush on me," he said with a grin.

Abby's jaw dropped and she huffed something about his "intolerable ego" until she saw the barely restrained glee in his eyes.

Then her gorgeous lips quirked at the edges, too. "You really enjoy getting me worked up, don't you?"

Reece took that as his cue, and stepped around the tree to pull her up close. "You have no idea," he said, serious now as he dipped in for another kiss.

"You're wicked," she said against his mouth, a little breathless. Her cheeks were flushed, her eyes bright, and Reece couldn't seem to get enough of taking her in.

"I know," he admitted. He seemed to be having especially wicked thoughts at the moment.

"I kind of like it," she said with a grin that made his heart flip inside his chest. "But I…I've never done this," she said, looking nervous.

His eyebrows flew up. He was pretty certain that… but was he wrong? "You mean you've never, uh—"

"Oh, no! I've had sex, sure. But never when I knew it was going to end before it started. Never without at least the vague promise of something more that could happen," she said, and then broke away, looking embarrassed.

"We have a relationship, Abby. We have history, even. We're friends. That won't change."

She smiled a little. "It's already changed. We were barely friends in high school, and we've barely started a friendship now. We're leaping right into being lovers."

He knew she was right, but didn't say a word.

"I want you," she admitted. "But I don't know if I can get into this knowing you're going to sell this place and leave. I know it's stupid, and unsophisticated, but I...um, I—"

Don't want to get hurt, he finished for her in his head.

"I know, Abby. I understand," he said, though he didn't want to. He wanted Abby more than he wanted just about anything except getting back in a car, but he didn't want to hurt her, either.

She wasn't like the women he took to bed and found gone in the morning. She wasn't just using him for a thrill or some notoriety. Abby was the kind of woman you took to bed and then woke up with in the morning— every morning—for a long time.

And he wasn't that guy. Maybe someday, but not now.

"It's sweet, actually," he said, closing the gap between them and pulling her into the circle of his arms. "I can't make any promises about anything, Abby, I can only be as upfront as possible. I want you, too, a lot. But it's your choice, okay?"

She nodded against his chest, her small hands moving over his back, making him crazy, but he reined in his desire.

"Thanks, Reece. I wish I could—"

"It's okay, really. How about we finish these trees?" he said cheerfully, planting a kiss on her hair and wondering if that was the last time he'd ever have Abby in his arms.

Reece exhaled softly. How could she sleep through that,
he wondered, watching Abby's chest rise and fall, and
resisted that need he had. Once she woke, how would he
tell her . . .

6

ABBY WRENCHED UPWARD, an unfamiliar noise pulling
her out of a restless dream.

The thud sounded again, and she sat up, hand to her
slamming heart. Looking at the clock, she saw it was
two-thirty in the morning. She'd only been sleeping for
a few hours. Living alone for several years now had
fine-tuned her senses to any noise in the house at night,
and she listened closer.

She didn't need to wonder if she had imagined it when
it was followed by a large crash, and glass breaking. She
leapt from the bed, opening her door to peek down the
hall toward Reece's room, but didn't see him. Had he
slept through the noise? Heard it at all?

Moving on tiptoe down the hall, she stopped by his
door, lifting her hand, then pausing. She couldn't knock
if there was an intruder downstairs, they might hear.

She pushed Reece's door open just slightly, poking
her head into the dark room.

"Reece?" she whispered as loudly as she dared.

A loud shout met her whisper, making her jump out
of her skin, but also launching her inside the room and

closing the door behind her. She saw immediately that the noise she'd heard hadn't been from an intruder, but from Reece, who had knocked the hurricane lamp off of his nightstand. He still appeared to be sleeping, and not well.

Venturing toward the bed, she bit her lip in concern.

"Reece, are you okay?"

He twisted in the sheets, as if trying to push them off, though he couldn't. He was murmuring, then shouting again, then whimpering in a way that told her he was in some kind of pain—or dreaming about it. She rushed to the side of the bed and put a calming hand on his shoulder, saying his name again, only to have him wrench away. He started saying things, his tone low and business-like, something with numbers and other mumbled words she couldn't understand.

Silver light shone through the window, and she could see his face was contorted in the agony of his dream and didn't know what to do. Then her eye caught sight of a small bottle on the dresser. She picked it up and held it close to the window—sleep aids. Those would knock him out and she probably didn't stand much chance of waking him up, she figured.

Still, she couldn't just leave him here like this, even if it was just a dream. Scooting into the empty space next to him, Abby knew she was playing with fire— especially when she realized he wasn't wearing anything but his briefs.

"God help me," she muttered, but settled down next to him and cuddled up behind, hoping to offer some kind of comfort. Maybe she could not let him be alone through the worst of it and then go back to her room.

Reece would never know. She rubbed his back with her palm, hoping to soothe, and after a few minutes, he did seem to quiet down. Her own body relaxed and her breathing returned to almost normal. Except that she was laying here in bed with a mostly naked, absolutely gorgeous man—still, she focused on just helping him back into a restful place.

Soon, his breathing evened, the mumbling stopped and his tight muscles softened under her hands.

"That's better," she said, intending to go back to her own room, but she was warm, comfortable and exhausted.

It didn't take much for her to drift off, too.

REECE WAS HAVING THE time of his life.

All drivers dreamed of the perfect race, and in his case, he was living the dream.

He was strapped into his Ferrari F60 so tightly that he could only just about breathe. The heat was intense, the wind bruising and the G-forces flattened him against the seat.

He was in sheer heaven—and he was in second place.

There was nothing in the universe except for his car, the road and the car in front of him. Adrenaline fueled his laserlike focus, strategy a constant clicking in his brain. Second would be his best in a World Cup race, but second wasn't good enough. Reece was pulling out all the stops and racing for first.

It had been raining. The roads were wet, but that was

nothing. He knew this car like his own body, and when he was driving it, there wasn't any difference between the two, the way he saw it.

He edged up on his competitor. Overtaking wasn't common on Formula One tracks, but he had a shot as they came around the final turn. He hit the accelerator as they rounded, positioning himself to make the most of the aerodynamics of the high-tech car he drove. The back wheel of the guy in front of him was spinning close by when Reece heard the whining noise, but he didn't catch on at first that something was wrong. He'd blown out the front driver's side tire.

He'd skipped that last pit stop. A calculated risk. A mistake.

His car could go on three tires in some conditions, but not rounding a curb, not at his speed, not on wet roads. His mind didn't anticipate the worst—he adjusted and focused on cold calculation of how to maneuver, still thinking about the win as he felt himself propel sideways, lurching hard.

Reece sometimes felt like he was flying when he drove, but something told him that for a second, he was actually airborne.

Everything was black, and then it was very, very bright.

The pain was intense, and he was trapped. He fought to get out, at least, he thought he did. He had no idea where he even was.

He couldn't seem to open his eyes, no matter how hard he tried. He wanted to speak but couldn't, and while there was noise in his head that wouldn't stop, he couldn't make out anything understandable.

Panic set in, fear clawing at him, and he tried to calm down, but it just made it worse. He lunged forward, reaching out, trying to get through the blinding brightness, the deafening noise, but he couldn't.

Was this what dying was like?

His heart felt as if it would explode from his chest when he felt something, finally. Someone touched him, and he reached, finding a hand he could grab on to. He held it like it was his only connection to life, and maybe it was.

He still couldn't speak, or hear, but he could touch.

His heartbeat slowed, the panic subsiding slightly. He was alive, connected to something.

Not alone.

For that moment, it was enough.

BEFORE SHE EVEN REALIZED IT, Abby opened her eyes to the soft, pre-dawn light, and to Reece's silver eyes watching her.

"Change your mind?" he said softly.

"Hmm?" she said, not sure what he was saying, or why he was in her bed, or... Her eyes flew open and she started to push up, but Reece's arm was over her, holding her snug against him.

"Steady," he said.

Morning brain-fog assaulted her, and she fought for words, but ended up sputtering, becoming increasingly aware of the warm, hard male body aligned with hers, both buried under the soft quilt and blankets.

"You were dreaming," she finally managed to say. "You broke your lamp. I thought you were an intruder," she explained, hoping he was awake enough to interpret her garbled, simple sentences.

As she shifted, it brought her closer to him and she knew he was *very* awake.

"You thought there was someone in the house, so you decided to crawl into bed with me?" he asked, his brow furrowed.

"No, I thought there was an intruder, but when I came to get you, I saw you had broken your lamp and were having a nightmare. Do you remember?"

He shook his head, then closed his eyes. "Vaguely. I've had it before, or other nightmares anyway. I don't know if it's the same one. I can never remember the details."

"You were thrashing around, so obviously it was... bad. I tried to wake you up, but you were out cold, so I thought maybe if I just sat with you for a while you'd be okay," she said, shrugging.

"You could have been hurt. Stepped on glass," he said, frowning.

"I was fine. You were the one hurting, apparently."

"And you helped," he said softly, looking at her strangely, like he was remembering something, but he didn't say anything, so she did.

"I meant to go back to my room, and then I guess I fell asleep."

"I see," he said, his eyes warm on her face.

"I should probably go," she said.

"Do you really want to?"

Did she?

Of course she did, but...but what?

All of her reservations seemed so flimsy. Sure, she

might get hurt, but she was a big girl. This was her chance to experience something wonderful, and there might never be another chance.

Reece would sell this winery, leave, and the odds were that she'd never see him again, except on TV.

Already, it hurt her heart a little to think about that, but so what? She'd survive, and she'd have some great memories. Maybe it was impossible to live your fantasies without some risk of being hurt. Maybe that was the price.

"No, I really don't," she said.

"Good, because I really want you to stay."

Her decision made, she smiled and slid her arm around him, too, enjoying how he pressed fully against her in a move that left her in no doubt that he wanted her—a lot.

The look of sheer hunger on his face made reason disappear. His lips were just a scant breath from hers, and she could hardly believe this was truly happening.

"Here's the thing, sweetheart," he said against her lips. "I don't care if an asteroid hits outside the window, nothing is interrupting us this time."

"Got it, no asteroids," she managed to say before he was kissing the life out of her, pushing her back until she was pinned between the warm, soft mattress and about six feet of hard, delicious man.

His mouth rubbed over hers erotically as he stopped to nip at her lower lip, his tongue darting out to lick the spot he bit before plunging deeper.

She arched into him, kissing him back with every ounce of passion she'd been holding back, tasting him as deeply as he tasted her. The faint scent of cedar, pine and smoke clung to his body from the night before, and she inhaled, loving how it mixed with his natural manly scent.

She barely recognized herself as she clung to him, wrapping a leg around his hip, arching into his hardness, rubbing and moaning into his mouth. She enjoyed sex, but she'd never felt so voracious about it. But right now, she wanted skin-on-skin, and pushed at the elastic band of the shorts between them.

He was of like mind, sliding his shorts off, then reaching for the edge of her flimsy cotton nightgown and pushing it upward until there wasn't anything hiding her from his gaze.

"Oh, sweetheart, this has been so worth waiting for," Reece said as he took her in. His hands drifted over her, learning her softness, studying her body so intently that she would have felt self-conscious if his touches weren't rendering her mindless.

"Um, I'm on birth control and I'm, you know, healthy. I haven't been with anyone in a while," she admitted, feeling a little awkward. But while they were old friends, they were new lovers, and certain things had to be said.

He nodded while nibbling at her shoulder, sending shivers everywhere.

"Me, too. Like I mentioned earlier, there's been no one since before the accident, and I've been thoroughly checked for everything with all of the time I spent in hospitals," he whispered against her ear.

She remembered how hard and urgent he'd been the day before when she'd stroked him to orgasm in the kitchen, and it was enough to make her shudder, reaching for him, wanting to make it happen again. The idea that she was his first lover after such a long time was important to her. Maybe that meant he wouldn't forget her later, either.

"Good, so we know we don't have to worry about *any* interruptions," she said with a smile.

She didn't want anything between them, and let him know by reaching down to find him, closing her fingers around him with a sigh of satisfaction. She opened her thighs and used her hand to slide him against her already slick sex, arching and then closing her legs to trap him there.

"I love how you feel next to me," she said, moving her hips against him, enjoying the slippery friction of their bodies. "But I bet it's not as good as you'd feel inside me."

"You make it tough to go slow," he said, pushing against her, sliding along the wet V of her flesh in a way that made her whimper and dig her fingers into his shoulders.

"Who wants slow?" she said, biting his shoulder. "Aren't you supposed to like speed?"

She yelped and then laughed as he found a ticklish spot and capitalized on it, then grabbed her hands and pinned them up over her head. She struggled slightly, and he could see it just excited her more when he pressed down, holding her in place.

Another little discovery about Abby.

"Now I've got you right where I want you," he said with a delicious smile. "And I plan to take my time. Maybe some guys make love like they race, but I think women and wine are more alike, they need to be savored," he said against her lips, catching her lower one between his teeth, then drawing it in and sucking before taking her whole mouth in a deep, carnal kiss. "We have time. Let's get to know each other," he said softly.

"But I want—"

"I know, me, too, and we'll get there. Promise," he said.

"You're such a tease," she accused, the last word ending on a moan as he ran his tongue along the shell of her ear, his cock still prodding and sliding along her sex, but not even coming close to where she wanted him.

"Can't help it when it comes to you," he said, moving lower to draw a nipple between his teeth, nipping lightly and making her arch, the slight pain making the drawing pleasure of his mouth a moment later even more intense.

He let her arms go and looked at her, his voice stern.

"Leave your hands there. Don't move them. I want to find out what you like, what you want," he said, his hands moving over her experimentally, lingering in places that made her react, moving on past the ones that didn't. "But if you move, I have to stop."

She nodded, moaning a little.

He was studying her body the way he must have studied a race course, or more accurately, tasting her like a good wine, she thought hazily, too immersed in sensation to argue. She'd been *done* plenty of times, but she'd never been paid attention to like this.

He dragged his lips down the inside of her thigh, and worked his way back up, nudging her legs apart with his shoulders.

His tongue found her, but only lightly, flicking at her clit, a butterfly touch that had her nearly screaming, writhing on the bed.

"Reece, please, I need you," she said, panting, but she obeyed, leaving her hands where he'd put them. It was driving her crazy, in the best possible way.

He licked her a little harder this time, and his fingers found their way inside of her—one, then two and then, making her eyes widen, another teased the other opening to her body, penetrating slightly. She tensed at the unexpected sensation, then relaxed. Her entire body shivered with the pleasure of his fingers and mouth everywhere.

"That feels so good," she said.

"And this?" he whispered against her sex, so softly she wasn't sure he really said anything before he kissed her again on pulsing, sensitive flesh.

"Yes," she said desperately, wanting more of everything, thrusting against him. "Please," she begged.

Reece was someone she'd known for so long, but she knew in that instant that she didn't know anything about him at all. He seemed to know what she fantasized about, what she wanted that maybe she didn't even know to ask for. He continued to press, to lick and to thrust until she cried out, arching off the bed, her body bent in ecstasy.

He moved back up, and levered over her, pulling her legs up over his shoulders.

"I need this so much," he said roughly, staring down into her face as he poised himself before her, rubbing and teasing her sex with his cock until both of them were mindless. When she was about to beg, he eased forward, sliding inside and filling her deeply, adjusting her legs so that he could go even deeper.

Oh, thank you, Abby thought, her entire body expressing a sigh of wonder as he started moving.

"You're so wet," he said, his jaw tight with the effort of control he was exerting. "So hot inside," he said, continuing to describe what he felt, what he wanted to do to her, in exacting detail until she wanted to just beg him to make it all real.

There was little she could do to control the pace at her angle, so she traced her hands and lips over hard lines of his chest, shoulders and hips. Every muscle was tense as he rocked into her in a steady rhythm.

She ran her fingers over his scars, exploring the different textures of his skin, then across the light hair on his chest, and over male nipples that beaded, drawing a groan from him as she pinched.

"You moved your hands," he said breathlessly.

"Do you mind?"

"Not at all."

He turned his face to the side, planting wet kisses on the side of her knee, and she whimpered as the sensation traveled all the way back down through her thighs to the eddy of pleasure between her legs.

It was all too good, but she needed more. She was so close, and reached down to touch him as he moved in and out, her fingers firm around the base of his erection.

"That's so hot, Abby," he said, watching.

She pressed on her clit then, rubbing, knowing what she needed and liking the way he watched so greedily. Hot sensation immediately coursed through her body, everything tightening, her muscles clenching down on his cock so hard it almost ached.

"Oh, yeah, Abby," he ground out, thrusting faster, deeper.

Suddenly all of the tightness melted, her climax overcoming her and drawing him along as well. Abby had never felt anything quite so pure in her life, she was sure of it.

Minutes later, Reece released her legs and fell to her side, pulling her over next to him as they both caught their breath, calming down from what Abby was sure had to be the most intense, incredible sex she'd ever had.

"I may not be able to move from this bed today," she said jokingly, though when she did try to move her leg, it felt like spaghetti. Her muscles felt as if they actually had melted.

"You'll get no arguments from me," Reece said with evil glee, propping up on one elbow at her side. He ran his finger along her sternum, down her belly, and stopped at the edge of her sex. "I thought about tying you to it at one point."

She was surprised, then she smiled.

"Maybe we could take turns."

"Sounds like a plan."

"I still can't feel my legs," she admitted, laughing.

"I'm a bit dizzy myself, but even so, I want more," he said, leaning in for a kiss.

"Me, too," she said, touching his face, running her finger along his lips. He darted his tongue out to taste her. "I want more, too."

"We can do anything," he said. "Everything. What-ever you want or need. Just say so."

In the years since her few crazy experiences in col-lege, her lovers had been nice but uncreative men, the sex more or less vanilla, and she hadn't realized how many fantasies she had packed away. If Reece was willing to explore them with her…?

"Maybe I should write up a list, you know, like for Santa. All the things I want you to do to me, and what I'd like to do to you," she said naughtily, grinning.

"Hmm…that could be interesting. We could make it our goal to make sure every item is attended to," he said, trailing his hand over her breast, in long strokes up and down her torso, down her arm, back up again, back over her breast until she trembled.

She wanted him again, right now. Amazing.

"Roll over."

"Why?"

"Just do it," he said, commanding but gentle.

With a little shiver of pleasure, she did, snuggling down into the soft material of his comforter. It was warm and soft, smelling like sex, and she was in heaven.

Reece pushed up, balancing himself as he levered over her, straddling the backs of her thighs, and then she felt the next-best thing to sex that she could imagine as his hands slid up either side of her spine and continued to massage in slow, thorough motions.

"That feels amazing…where did you learn to give massages?" she said.

"Here and there…but giving a massage can feel as good as getting one," he responded.

As he worked her neck, she sighed. "Somehow I doubt

that," she said on another sigh, followed by a moan as he leaned forward and was inside of her again, moving in a lazy rhythm that matched the motion of his hands.

She'd never even imagined so much physical sensation being possible. He kept rubbing, moving over her and inside of her until she was clawing her fingers into the quilt and rotating her hips beneath him. It was so slow, it was torture. It was perfect.

His hands slipped down to work their magic on her derriere, massaging and squeezing. She pushed up on her elbows, thrusting back against him, seeking more. He kept up the constant gentle rhythm, a steady beat of pleasure, as if making love to her was a song. She fell to the bed again, giving herself up to him and enjoying every second of it.

He never stopped touching her, through her orgasm and then through his own. Abby drifted off to sleep later, thinking that she'd definitely given herself the best Christmas present she could have ever imagined.

REECE HADN'T FELT SO good since, well, since he couldn't remember. He'd slept some more after making love to Abby, and it had been a deep, dreamless, drugless sleep, which he hadn't known in quite some time.

When he saw the mess he'd made of the nightstand, breaking one of his mother's antique lamps, he wished he could remember the dream. The only impression he was ever left with was that of being horribly trapped, dying, until someone touched him. Abby. As if she had reached directly into his terror and made it stop.

He cleaned the mess while she was still sleeping, liking the way her foot dangled over the edge of his bed.

A silly thing to trip his heart rate, but nearly enough to make him slide his hand up the arch and crawl back in with her. He'd lived in France too long not to have developed at least a little bit of a romantic streak, he guessed, as he smiled at her pretty pink toes.

Instead, he pulled himself away and pushed through a punishing workout, especially after the wonderful but rich dinner Abby had cooked the night before.

He'd been way off the nutritional regimen that he usually adhered to during the year, but things were always a little more slack around the holidays—more sweets, more wine—and so he had to make up for it with exercise.

Racing was more punishing on the body that most people imagined, requiring a lot of strength to turn a car that was pushing down three Gs. He had to work twice as hard now.

He was feeling strong today, though. Energized. There was no numbness, no pins and needles. A second round of push-ups was interrupted by the doorbell, and he went quickly to answer, hoping not to wake Abby. Much to his surprise, Charles stood at the door, frowning through the ring of the wreath Abby had hung over the panes of glass the day before.

"What the hell is all of this?" Charles asked, looking back at the trees set up on the large front lawn as he stepped inside.

"Good morning to you, too," Reece said dryly, not offering to take Charles's coat. "To what do I owe this impromptu visit so very early in the morning?"

Charles glared. "It's not impromptu—we have an appointment with the Keller rep in a half hour, and I thought we had talked about staging? Why all the trees and lights? What's going on?"

Reece had been remiss in telling Charles about Abby moving in, and so he proceeded to do that, watching the real estate agent's face redden as he spoke. When he was done, Charles didn't say anything, but went outside, peering over across the field past the trees on the lawn to the blackened buildings on the hill before he stomped back in.

"Okay, okay, let's not panic. This could work for us."

"What do you mean?"

"Well, we'd talked about her selling, in a package deal with you, right? Maybe now that would be even more appealing—certainly more appealing than having that right in the line of view from the front door. And that barn—that alone would bring down the property value—"

Reece held up his hand. "Stop right there. The barn is fine, she keeps her horses there, and I can guarantee you there's no way she's selling. And I know she'd regret causing us any inconvenience by having her home almost burnt to the ground," he said, not bothering to hide his sarcasm, "but I'm letting her work through the end of the holiday season here, period. It's good for us, too, since I have inventory to clear out."

"So why all the trees? You selling those, too, now?"

"It's for a tasting event. They are having a tree-decorating contest and giving away a case of wine and a weekend at their inn, when it's rebuilt, to the winner."

"Cute. But we can't have this all going on while we're trying to show the place—she'll have to be willing to clear out when we're bringing prospective buyers through."

Reece pushed a hand though his hair, and didn't have time to argue as another car pulled up in front of the house, and a burly man in a black suit approached the house. He stopped and looked out over the land, and Reece could see him bulldozing just by how he surveyed the property.

Reece didn't bother to grab a jacket and the three of them walked the property, the Keller rep obviously liking what he saw. Reece liked what he saw, too. It had been a while since he'd walked the land, taking in the view of crystal blue Cayuga Lake, breathing in the clean air.

Standing among the rolling hills of vines, snow bright on the branches of trees that marked the boundaries, he wondered how he'd never noticed how similar the place was to where he lived in France. Just as beautiful, just as pristine. Showing it to the Keller sales rep was like seeing it himself for the first time.

"We'd be willing to offer you top dollar, Winston. This is a great location, driving distance to the city, and having bought it from a famous local celebrity can only add to its draw. We're thinking we could use the local vineyards as a jumping-off point, give the development a vineyard theme, all of the streets named after certain kind of grapes, maybe name the place Vineyard Hills, or something to that effect," the man said, obviously getting way ahead of himself.

"Yeah, I always wondered about that," Reece said. "Why developers come into a place, clear out all the pine trees and then name them all after what they cleared out…"

Charles glared, but the Keller rep laughed and slapped

him on the shoulder. Reece had expected some slimy sales guy, but this man was local and down-to-earth in a way a lot of central New York people were. He didn't take offense at all.

"Just the way of the business, I guess."

Reece liked him, which made it harder to think of Keller as so bad. He was a businessman looking to do business, and so why did it all irritate him so much?

"The property down the line might be for sale as well," Charles added as they stood on the front porch again, nodding down toward Abby's place. "Maybe we could work out some kind of package deal?"

"Charles—" Reece interrupted, but he didn't get far.

"I'd have to talk to the boss, but that could be a very appealing prospect," Keller agreed. "I know you want to sell, and we'd be happy to talk about some kind of package, but we're also looking at a prime piece of property over on Kueka, so we'll decide which way we want to go, but we won't wait indefinitely," he said.

Reece nodded and bit his tongue as he noticed movement inside the window. Abby was up. He wasn't going to get into this now. They shook hands with a promise to stay in contact, and the Keller guy left.

Charles looked disgusted. "He wants it, Reece, and if you know what's smart, you'll move your friend out of here as soon as possible and off-load this place, and hers, if you can get it. If not, you're going to have it shackled to your ankle for some time, or take a huge loss," he warned before walking down toward his own car.

Reece's good morning vibe evaporated, and he stood on the porch watching Charles leave. There was no way he was asking Abby to leave before the holiday season was over, and he had to hope that wouldn't get in the way of a deal. He knew he should be putting the sale first—Abby was a big girl—but he'd made a promise, and he intended to keep it.

Walking back into the house, the warmth and the scent of coffee and pine trees wrapped around him in welcome. The strong sense of being *home* was disconcerting, making him stop in the entryway and looked around the room. Maybe Charles was right about the staging. When the house was empty, his parents gone, no decorations, he could look at it as a building to be sold.

Now, with Abby's coat over the back of the chair, her bag on the table, the tree in the corner, and some boxes of ornaments still stashed by the wall, the place looked…lived in.

Was he making a mistake?

He heard her talking in the other room, on the phone, and wondered how what had been so black and white just the day before was now not clear at all.

7

ABBY AWAKENED FEELING like a cat, warm, loose-muscled and well-tuned, but the minute her feet had hit the floor, doubts had set in and chaos followed her every footstep right into the shower.

She'd slept with Reece. That seemed like a tremendous understatement. The luscious, carnal hours made her warm with arousal even now and blew her previous idea of what "good sex" could be right out of the water.

It had been *great* sex.

Still, in the very bright light of day that was glaring off the snow-covered ground, they would have to face each other and the realities between them.

The morning began with a second call for Reece from Danielle, which Abby overheard while making coffee. The woman sounded irritated as she left her message on the machine, and guilt assailed Abby for forgetting Danielle's first one.

Jealousy also kicked in, and Abby knew she couldn't afford that. It was just sex, and being jealous wasn't part of the bargain. She'd make sure he knew about Danielle's calls as soon as she saw him, which made her wonder where he was.

She looked out the front window when she heard voices and saw a black sedan parked out front, Keller Industries written in neat, white lettering on one door.

Her hands turned cold as she saw the three men round the corner of the tasting rooms and come up to the house. They stood on the porch, apparently enjoying their conversation, looking over at *her* property, once, at least, their expressions speculative.

Coffee turned to acid in her stomach as she watched Reece smile and shake hands with the guy from Keller.

Her cell phone rang, and she turned toward the table near the Christmas tree they had decorated together the night before, her mind still on Reece even as the speaker on the other end addressed her. The whole incredible evening was starting to feel like a lie, a huge mistake.

Then, what she was hearing made those concerns seem like mere annoyances, her mind snapping to attention. "What do you mean the insurance payments have been halted?" she asked, setting her cup down on the counter before she dropped it.

"The complete fire investigator's report showed that while the fire was caused by an electrical short, it came closer to the wall by where one of your trees was plugged in, not at the source of your wiring problem in the ceiling."

Abby blinked. "So?"

"There is some indication that the wires could have been tampered with when the tree was set up."

Abby's jaw dropped, and her mind blanked with disbelief.

"Are you saying you think the fire was intentionally set?"

"It's not certain, but any doubt creates the need for a larger investigation before we can pay out. We have to make sure there's no fraud concern, you understand."

He said it so politely, accusing her of setting fire to her own home, as if it was just business.

"They're bringing in another investigator to make a new report, but until then, any progress on rebuilding or payment has to be stopped. We're very sorry for the inconvenience," the insurance agent said.

"How long will this take?" Abby knew the fire was an accident, but any delay on scheduling new construction would further eat into her reopening the following year.

"The investigator will be there Monday, but the report could take a few weeks. With the holidays, everything is slowed down, but I'm sure they'll get on it as soon as possible. Can you also supply them with the names of the company that brought in the trees?"

"You think they might have tampered with my wiring? I can assure you, they didn't. No one did. This was just an accident. My family has done business with them for years. This is just some stupid misunderstanding."

"Either way, they'll be conducting interviews and getting all of the information they can."

Abby was numb as she hung up the phone and heard the front door open.

Reece.

She had to compose herself, to hide her distress. She didn't want to talk about this new mess with him right now.

But as soon as she moved, her phone rang again.

Looking down, she closed her eyes when she saw her father's name on the caller ID.

Tears stung behind her eyelids seeing her dad's name. She wished so much they were here, and at the same time, she was glad they weren't. In spite of what she had to tell them, she was relieved to hear her father's voice on the line when she picked up the call.

"Hi, Dad," she said, her voice breaking immediately even though she promised herself she'd remain stalwart. She tried, only crying a little as she told them everything, including the new trouble.

As Reece and Hannah predicted, her parents were shocked, but their first concern was her safety, and they were clearly not as worried about the property, to an extent that left Abby somewhat surprised.

"I guess I thought you'd be more upset," she said to her dad, somewhat confused. "You built this place. You devoted everything to it."

"Oh, honey, we are, but more so that you have to deal with all of this alone. Should we come home?"

"No, no, please don't. I'm not alone. I have Hannah, and Reece has been so generous," she said, wanting them to know she wasn't completely on her own, as much as she missed them. "And besides, there's not much I can do until the insurance works itself out, I guess, and they do this new investigation."

"Well, that's just absurd," her mother said, joining in the call on conference. "Dad will make a call to Harold this afternoon," her mom assured. Harold was their long-time insurance agent who had retired, but probably still would have some good advice.

"I'm glad you're taking it okay," Abby said. "I was so worried about telling you."

"Sweetheart, all we care about is that you are unhurt, and it's so good to know Beau and Buttercup and the other pets are safe. When you see the kinds of things we've seen here in Haiti, helping people rebuild when they have so little, or just getting clean water running, it tends to help straighten out priorities," her mom added, and Abby heard her father's murmured assent in the background.

"You just say the word, and we'll come back if you need us. You're our first priority and always will be," her mom said.

"I'm fine, Mom, really. I'm good here at Reece's through the season, and hopefully after that, things will be more settled. I can stay with Hannah until the house is back to rights," she added.

"I'm so impressed that Reece stepped up like that," her mother said. "Not that he wasn't always a nice young man, and I think he did have a bit of a crush on you," she said, and Abby's eyes widened as she heard the smile in her mom's voice.

"Reece? Have a crush on me? Hardly," she scoffed.

"He was a handsome boy," her mom continued. "I take it he's recovering from that awful accident? And his father is doing well?"

Abby filled her mom in on everything. Okay, not *everything*, although she had that sneaking feeling that her parents could sense something more than being neighborly was between her and Reece. She did nothing to encourage that idea—there was no point when she and Reece were clearly just having a holiday fling that would be over soon enough.

She stared at the blinking red light on the phone to her left. Danielle.

Nevermind, that. She was here, now, and some woman an ocean away was not her concern. She felt marginally better. At least telling her parents hadn't been as terrible as she thought it might be, and her parents were right.

When she hung up, Abby felt more in control of things. As her parents pointed out, there were people in the world with much bigger problems than hers. She was alive, healthy and able to deal with whatever life put in front of her.

She wished she felt so confident about her emotions concerning Reece as she heard him in the front room. Taking another deep breath, she went out to meet him. No sense in avoiding it.

She stepped through the hall and stopped in her tracks the minute their eyes met, her composure flying out the window as she remembered every single touch, kiss and more. She wanted to cross the room and throw herself up against him, to feel the warm solidity of his body and forget everything else.

His brow lowered, and he looked at her, concerned. Probably because she was just standing there like a moron.

"Abby, you okay?"

"I talked to my folks" was the first thing out of her mouth, and while she didn't move, he did, crossing the room to pull her in. He was so warm, even though he was only wearing a heavy sweater coming in from outside.

"How did it go?" he asked.

She nodded, her cheek rubbing against the rough wool that covered his chest, his warmth seeping through, comforting her.

"They took it better than I imagined. I guess they've seen so much devastation, they have a different perspective on things," she said.

This wasn't going at all as she had planned. It was wrong to feel so good being able to talk to him while he stood there, holding her. His hands were rubbing over her back, and the comfort started to turn hot as sparks of desire leapt between them.

Should they talk about the night before? What was there to say? She pushed back gently, trying to rein her reactions in.

"Um, I don't know if you noticed, but you have a message on the kitchen phone. And I forgot to tell you last night," she said, feeling her cheeks heat annoyingly.

"A woman, Danielle, called yesterday, and I picked up the phone without thinking, and I promised her I would give you the message, which she said you would know who it was, and then I forgot to let you know, with everything that…happened," she babbled, lowering her gaze to his mouth.

He had such a great mouth.

"Danielle called?" he said then, sounding pleased. Her heart sank.

"Yeah, um, I just thought you should know. I didn't know if you checked the machine, it's hard to notice that little blinking light on your parents' phone unless you are standing in there right by the sink, and so I wanted to make sure you knew," she said, babbling again in the face of her discomfort. "I'm sorry I forgot yesterday."

Was the smile on his face because of Danielle?

"No need to apologize. I miss calls on that all the time—I'm surprised she didn't call my cell, but she might not have international minutes, I guess. Thanks," he said, not elaborating. Why would he?

"Old friend?" she asked spontaneously when he didn't offer more, then bit her lip and looked away, regretting giving in to the urge.

"Yeah," Reece said easily, apparently thinking nothing of it. "Actually, her brother, Gerard, was a driver and a good friend of mine since I'd moved to Europe. He was killed in a nonracing crash a few years ago."

Abby lifted a hand to her mouth. "Oh, no, that's awful. I'm so sorry."

"Yeah, it was hard on all of us. He was a great guy, helped me get into the sport. Danielle was his only sibling, and we spent some time together after he was gone. She helped me a lot last year," he said, shaking his head, remembering.

"There were days I might not have gotten up to bother with my physical therapy if she hadn't been there, cursing me out in three languages if I whined about it," he said, laughing at the memory.

Abby was silent. And she thought they had history? How could she compete with something like that? Danielle had been with Reece day after day through a time in his life he didn't really even want to talk to Abby about. It made her feel on the outside, in spite of the closeness they'd shared just hours before.

"I'm glad you had someone there for you," she said

slowly, and she meant it, even if it cost her something to admit.

"I guess I was, too, even if at the time I didn't always like her very much for ranting at me and pushing me. I guess she figured she'd fill in for Gerard, at least, that's what Tomás told me once."

"Tomás?"

"Danielle's husband. She spent so much time at the hospital with me, he said he felt like a single parent," Reece said. "But I was grateful for her pushing. She convinced me I could do anything I wanted to do, even go back to racing. It took some of the worry off of my parents, too, knowing she was there."

Danielle's husband. The words rang in Abby's mind. She'd been thinking the sexy-sounding French woman had been a lover, picturing a svelte vixen who warmed Reece's bed when he was in Europe.

In fact, she sounded like a good friend, and a wonderful person—a much better person than Abby felt like at the moment.

"Why are you frowning?" Reece asked, watching her closely.

"I, uh…never mind," she said, not about to confess that she'd been jealous of a woman she not only didn't know but had absolutely no good reason to be jealous of.

"I saw you were meeting with the Keller rep this morning. And the man you were at the café with the other day?" she asked, changing the subject.

His mouth flattened. "Yeah, he's interested, but we're not making any deals yet."

"Yet," she echoed softly. "When?"

"They haven't made a formal offer. They're considering a couple of other properties as well."

"Including mine?" she asked.

He blinked in surprise. "Why do you say that?"

"I happened to see you all looking over there, and the man you were with pointed to my buildings. So I wondered what that was about."

Reece was notably uncomfortable. He turned, talking as he randomly reorganized some boxes that were in the path of the hallway.

"They saw it and wondered about the fire," he explained haltingly, then sighed. "But, yes, it would be more attractive to them to get both properties in a package deal. They thought that since you had the fire, you might be interested in selling, too."

"I'm not."

"I told them that," he said, making eye contact. "I know you don't want to sell. I know this affects you, too, my selling. I can't promise I'm going to sell to someone you'll approve of—"

"Keller," she said woodenly.

"Maybe. If there are options, we can talk about them."

"Okay."

"But Abby?"

"Hmm?"

"I am going back to Europe and back to racing, sooner than later if I have my way. I need you to know that."

She knew it, but she couldn't help asking what was on her mind since she'd seen him in the café. "I thought the news said, I mean, they said the doctors said…" She faltered, hating to say it out loud.

"That my injuries were too severe, I know. That I would probably never make the full recovery needed to race again," he bit out, looking away, bitterness and determination carved into every line of his face. "I know what they say." He pushed a hand through his hair.

He looked so tense, she took a step closer, trying to find something encouraging to say. "Well, you seem pretty healthy to me," she said with a smile. "What are they waiting for?"

He looked up and seemed to relax a little.

"I have relapses, numbness, some pins and needles, and my reflex time has slowed down. I can build it back up if I can get back into proper training. The longer I'm here…"

She nodded, keeping her tone neutral. "The harder it is for you to get back in."

He sighed. "I'll be easily forgotten, replaced, if I don't get back in soon. I have to show them I can do it."

"Why?" Why did he want to return to a sport that almost killed him and might not take him back?

He stared at her in surprise. "I love it. It's the one thing I have ever really loved doing, really excelled at."

She frowned, thinking back. Reece had been an excellent student and athlete.

"I find that hard to believe."

"It's true. I was good at a lot of things, but nothing was my passion. Sometimes I ever wondered if I would have one. My dad would always say how he'd had wine in his blood and he felt so connected to this place. Ben knew what he wanted to do, to design golf courses, since he stepped foot on one when he was ten. I never had that focus, that desire, until I found racing. I can't even think of what else I would do with myself," he said, sounding slightly hollow, and her heart went out to him. "It's all I know."

"I can understand that," she said, and she did. She loved her home, her business, and she couldn't imagine any other work, either.

She took a deep breath, closing her eyes, then opening them again. "Give me a week. I'm meeting with Hannah to see if there's any way for me to liquidate assets and maybe buy you out. I don't know if it's possible, but maybe we could work something out, if you're willing."

He nodded. "I'd love you to have the place, and if there's a way we can do that, I'm all for it. I know my parents would be thrilled, too. We don't want to sell to Keller, but the market is so hard now, and we can't keep this place running for long."

"I'll do what I can," she said, but hope faded as she thought about the insurance money not coming through.

It had been feasible that she could have used that as a down payment, but she didn't tell Reece that. "And if we can't, and if you have to sell to Keller, do it. Maybe you can even leave earlier, get back to your life, your training," she said, proud of how calm she sounded.

"Trying to get rid of me, Abby?" He offered a small, slanted smile, but it didn't reach his eyes.

"No, but you obviously need to get back. The sooner the better, right?" She sounded brittle to her own ears.

He stood close again, and she resisted the urge to lift a hand, to touch him. How had this become so difficult so quickly?

"And until then?"

She didn't want to talk. She didn't want to debate the options and treat what was between them like a contract, discussing the terms and what-ifs.

She wanted him, and she had the chance to spend some time with him over the holiday. She'd be too busy to deal with a broken heart later, she figured.

Reaching up, she slid her hands around his neck, linking her arms behind and pulling his mouth down to hers.

"In the meantime, we have this," she said, kissing him until talking wasn't what either of them was interested in.

8

ABBY KNEW REECE WAS avoiding her, she just didn't know why.

In the three days since their talk, their last kiss—a kiss that hadn't led to a night in his bed—they'd both been busy and preoccupied.

When she was at the house, he seemed to be gone, and she was too busy even when he was there, working in the tasting room until late hours, getting things set up, preparing for the upcoming wedding and Christmas events.

As before, she'd come home to find him already in bed, his light shining under the closed door, or in the workout room going through the punishing routine that he did two or three times a day now. She didn't want to interrupt.

She hadn't slept well for those lonely nights, and so maybe this was best. She had too much happening to lose sleep over relationship drama.

Like right now, Abby was trying to get the supplies out to the yard where the Christmas trees waited. Hannah was supposed to have come with help an hour ago, but called to say she had a bad tire and had to have it changed before she could pick up their other part-timer for the day and get out there.

So Abby was on her own. Again. She didn't like to complain—she loved her work—but so much of it had come down on her shoulders recently, she was starting to feel it more than ever.

In a short while, the yard would fill with parents and children for the Christmas tree–decorating contest. Tasting was set up for the parents, with cases of both Maple Hills and Winston Vineyard wines up for first prize, with single bottles for second and third, along with fun prizes for the kids, who could also take part in a snowball-throwing contest and a snowman build-a-thon. The first-place winner would also get a free weekend at her inn next summer as a way to promote future business, and to ensure people would know she was rebuilding.

Boxes of lights, garland and unbreakable ornaments as well as popcorn were ready to be strung, along with other creative decorations that had to be hauled out to the yard and set up. Everything had to be ready to start just past noon. She'd been running behind all morning and could have used a hand, waiting for Hannah and her other helper.

Reece's truck was over by the barn, but she hadn't seen him yet. He had come in late the night before and was probably sleeping in. Besides, he'd been clear that he didn't want to be too involved with the everyday business of the winery. He was handling the Winston inventory and sales, and answered any questions she had, but otherwise, he stayed out of it.

Now that seemed to include her, too, apparently. She didn't understand it, but something had changed after their talk. Maybe he realized he'd made a mistake, or maybe he had simply gotten what he wanted.

She had, too, right? So why did it hurt so much now? She'd gone into it with her eyes open. They hadn't made any commitments. No promises. Reece had made it clear he was still poised to leave, and she had been the one throwing herself back at him. Maybe, in his way, he had been trying to back away, but she just didn't get it. Why couldn't he just tell her so instead of avoiding her? Or maybe he had only meant it to be a one-night thing, and she had misunderstood.

She was about to pick up another full box and bring it out to the yard when she heard footsteps, Reece coming down the creaky hardwood stairs from his room. He turned the corner, pausing when he saw her. She was grateful to see him, but also worried. He looked like he hadn't slept all night, either.

"Hey," she said, unable to ignore the way the brown hair mussed, the five o'clock shadow thick on his jaw. His body was probably still warm from sleep, and the magnetic pull toward him was hard to resist. But she did. She leaned down and picked up the box instead, holding it in front of her like a barrier.

"Hey," he said back, looking toward the kitchen.

"There's still coffee if you want some," she offered.

"Thanks," he said, taking a few steps in that direction, and she noticed him wince, a hitch on his left side.

"Are you okay?"

"I'm fine," he said. "Just had a rough night."

There was no warmth in his voice, and she felt

awkward and exposed standing there, even though she was dressed in her winter coat and sweater. None of it seemed enough to keep the hurt his tone caused from penetrating into her chest.

She told herself to stop being stupid. He'd had a bad night and was tired and a little grumpy, that was all. Maybe he just needed some downtime, or some fun.

"Okay, well, we have the tree-decorating contest today. It's going to be a good time, and you're welcome to join. In fact—"

"Listen, Abby, I don't think I can do this. It's too complicated," he said wearily.

"It's just trees, Reece, we're going to—"

"I don't mean the trees," he said abruptly and shuffled off into the kitchen.

Abby took the box outside without another word, hoping the cold slap of air on her cheeks would freeze the tears stinging behind her eyes. So, he had been trying to break things off, and she hadn't understood. Now she did.

Still, did he have to be so harsh? What had she done to deserve that?

Whatever warmth was between them seemed to have evaporated. Maybe it was better. Being together like they were would only make it harder, and she couldn't say he wasn't honest about things.

Yes, this was better, she thought, her heart aching as she dropped the box by the Christmas trees and turned to get another one, pulling her coat tighter as the sun dipped behind a cloud.

Then anger set in. He might be having a hard time of it, but that was no reason to treat her badly.

Whatever was going on, she deserved better treatment from him than being so easily dismissed, she thought as she walked back in for another box and stepped past them and into the kitchen instead. She stopped in the doorway, hearing two voices, realizing Reece had turned on the speakerphone.

She should leave, she thought, but her feet didn't seem to move.

"I can do it, Joe, give me a chance to show you. Whatever little things are still bugging me, I can ignore them. It's not a big deal," Reece said, tense.

"If it were just up to me, I'd give you a shot, but it's not. Something happens to that car this early in the game, I don't have to tell you how bad that would be. I'll be out of a job, and we'll both have lawsuits landing on us. The doc says no. Sorry to say it, but you're out, Reece. It's just a shitty break."

"I don't give a damn what he says, how the hell can he know what I'm able to do?" Reece's voice rose.

The other man sighed audibly over the phone. "Reece, you need to accept reality. It can't happen. You're one lucky bastard as it is, having survived that wreck. What's still wrong with your body is enough to take you out at two hundred if something goes wrong, and you know it. Why go take a second chance at killing yourself?"

"I'd be fine. Just let me do some test drives in January, I'll show you."

Abby's heart squeezed painfully for him; he wanted this so much, and it didn't sound like things were going his way.

"I'll see what I can do, Reece. But you haven't been

cleared on the post-traumatic stress issues, either. The doctor said you stopped the counseling."

Abby froze. PTS? She'd heard more about that in the news lately, with returning soldiers, but she hadn't thought about it in terms of things like a car accident. But it made perfect sense—anytime someone almost lost their life, especially if there were violent circumstances, post-traumatic stress would be an issue.

She put a hand to her lips. Maybe that was why Reece was acting so erratically, having nightmares and so forth. Her anger melted in the face of new information.

"I'm fine. Take my word for it."

"Well, the sponsors are looking at a new guy, an up-and-comer, got a hot record so far, and…"

Abby didn't hear the rest of what the guy had to say. She watched as Reece's head fell forward in a clear expression of his frustration and unhappiness at the news.

She took a step, then another, needing to comfort him in some way, his earlier surliness forgotten. None of that mattered. All that she cared about at the moment was being there for Reece, the way he'd been there for her lately.

REECE HAD SO MANY emotions crashing together inside of him, he didn't know which one to deal with first. Anger that they wouldn't listen and that the damned doctors wouldn't clear him. Betrayal that they wouldn't trust him to do what he was so good at doing, that they were just writing him off.

Fear that he'd never get to drive again, or maybe he

was way past fear and closer to panic. Joe said the team was already lining up someone new.

When he looked up from where he had braced his hands against the counter over a cooling cup of coffee and saw Abby looking at him with her heart in her eyes, he added embarrassment to the mix.

"Joe, I have to go. See what you can do, I'll be in touch," he said, hanging up abruptly.

"Reece…" she began.

"Eavesdropping, Abby?"

"No!" She closed her eyes, blowing out a breath. "I mean, not on purpose. I came back in to talk, and you were on the phone, and I just…heard," she explained.

"I see."

He'd knew that he'd growled at her when he came downstairs, still groggy from the painkillers he was taking to help him sleep through the pain in his left leg that had been torturing him for the last few days.

He hadn't touched Abby since their conversation about the sale, and he didn't intend to. While she had come to him even after he told her it could never be more than sex, he decided to put some distance between them, to cool things off, for both of their sakes. It didn't matter that he wanted more, too. He knew they were getting in too deep, too fast, and it wouldn't be good for either of them in the end. Better to hurt her now, the way he saw it.

He hadn't counted on it, but he missed her like hell, and that pissed him off, too, unaccountably. He'd avoided emotional complications with women, and this was why.

The first two nights he'd been awake, he'd only been

able to think about her being a few yards down the hall, and how much he wanted her. He'd paced, tossed and turned, worked out and then, probably due to anxiety and lack of sleep, his left side started acting up worse than ever.

So last night he'd turned to the painkillers to smother the pain, which was now accompanied by a burning sensation that was a new kind of agony. If it kept up, he knew he'd have to go in to see the doctors, but he was determined to make it stop or to learn to ignore it. He was trying hard to ignore it.

Abby chewed her lip, watching him, looking unsure. He grabbed the coffee and then set it down, his fingers curling tightly as he fought the urge to go to her, to smooth over his harsh words.

"I'm so sorry, Reece."

"For what?"

"That they don't want you to race anymore," she said, her words soft, pained, for him.

He frowned, not wanting her sympathy. That was the last thing he wanted. "Don't waste your pity on me, Abby. I am going to drive again, and soon."

"But he said—"

"I know what he said. They might have some new hotshot lined up, but I can talk to the sponsors myself. I have a strong record, a following, and there's nothing fans like more than a comeback. I will make a hell of a lot more money for them, and get more wins, than someone green out of the gate," he said, almost convincing himself.

"What about the post-traumatic stress?"

"That's nothing. A few nightmares, some lost sleep. It will pass. The rest I can handle."

"Maybe dismissing it too easily is part of the problem," she offered.

Reece put a hand up. Abby was a good friend who meant well, he knew, but her words got his back up. He wanted to keep their friendship in place, but he also wasn't going to have this conversation with her.

"Abby, listen. I care about you, and I want us to be friends, but there's a lot you don't know about me. I know my own limitations."

"You have to talk about it with someone," she countered.

"Not you."

"Why not?"

"Abby, we slept together. That doesn't give you a free pass into my life," he said. "Besides, it's not like you don't have your own agenda. The longer I stay, the better for you, putting off the sale, right?"

He regretted the words as they passed his lips, but was unable to resist the urge to push her away.

Why? Because she was right? Was Joe right, too?

He couldn't deal with it and turned to leave, surprised when he felt her hand on his arm, pulling him back around.

She was furious, her eyes were mossy green, darkened by emotion. Her hand left his arm to settle on her hip, but he'd missed her so much that even such a quick touch left its impression.

"Are you serious? You think I am sleeping with you to stall you from selling?"

He didn't, he never thought that, but he didn't say so. If she hated his guts, things would probably work out easier for both of them. She had enough to think about without worrying about his problems, too.

She shook her head in astonishment. "I'm not sure who that is more insulting toward, me or you," she said.

"I'm sorry, Abby, it's just that I've been here before. I've been with women who think sex is more, and I know the signs."

Now her mouth was gaping at him.

"Need an ego adjustment, Reece? I have a lot going on, and yes, I don't want you selling to Keller, but I've accepted that you might. I've known from the start what we have…had…was temporary. Don't think I am hanging my future on you. My future is over there." She pointed out the window to her winery, and he saw her hand tremble. She was clearly furious, and she was right.

"I'm sorry, Abby. I just didn't want you getting the idea that I would stay, or that sleeping together means more than it does."

She shook her head, looking at him like she'd never seen him before.

"Don't worry, Reece. As far as I'm concerned, it didn't mean a damned thing."

Reece closed his eyes, wishing he knew a better way to handle this, but he was fighting on so many fronts, he didn't know what else to do. He felt as if he was fighting the whole damned world and himself, and he was tired of it.

He started to say something, he wasn't even sure

what, but she'd already started to leave the room. He stepped forward, thinking about following, but instead he grabbed his jacket from the hook by the door and went out the back door to the barn with his cold coffee.

"HEY, WHERE'S REECE?" Hannah asked Abby, smiling at a young girl who stood with her father, waiting on a paper cup of hot chocolate. "Anything interesting progressing there?" she asked slyly.

The father took a small tasting glass of Baco Noir, and Hannah marked his plastic bracelet with a second check—no one got more than three tastings in the course of an hour, even if they spat between tastings, so that they were okay to drive when they left.

Abby hadn't filled in Hannah on everything going on, but that was because she had an event to focus on, which was good. Having a couple dozen people flying in every direction and Christmas trees being decorated kept her from dwelling on what had happened that morning.

She was still furious, though maybe with herself as much as anything. How could she have been so stupid?

"Hardly. He's around here somewhere," she said vaguely. Reece hadn't left, and he hadn't been in the house the last time she went inside, sparing them both another awkward moment.

She'd heard some noises coming from one of the barns, the sounds of power tools. He must be working on something, though she didn't go to find out what. She didn't care.

Well, the sad fact was that she *did* care, but she

had to stop. The ache that had been dully thudding in the background of her heart all afternoon became so sharp as she replayed his words in her mind that she swallowed hard and pushed it back down. This was not the time.

Hannah watched father and daughter walk away, her eyes clearly focused on the man's butt, distracting Abby enough to make her smile.

"Why are all the cute ones married?" her friend sighed. "What I wouldn't give for just one night of unbelievably hot sex right now."

Abby coughed, looking around to make sure none of the children or parents had overheard Hannah's heartfelt wish.

"Weren't you dating that lawyer?"

"Yeah, that was over weeks ago. He was boring. I could hardly get through dinner on our first date without falling asleep in my spaghetti. That was enough for me."

"Oh."

"Yeah. And it's getting pretty sparse out there. I can't date the guys I work with, of course, and most of the other men our age I've known since we were kids. If I slept with one of them, everyone in town would know and my mother would have us married."

Hannah sighed, pouring herself a larger glass of the noir. "What I need is some wild, kinky sex with someone who's not local. I'd settle for just one night with a guy whose mother or friends I might not bump into the next day at the store."

Abby shook her head, grimacing. "Watch what you wish for."

"I'm willing to risk it," Hannah said. "But I take it things fizzled between you and Reece?"

"More like they imploded," she said, closing her eyes at the hitch in her voice.

"Oh, no, honey…you fell for him, didn't you?"

"Not really. Well, a little," Abby admitted. "It's not like I am madly in love with him or going to jump off a cliff, but I thought we had something. Then he—he just decided that we didn't. I didn't see it coming, not really. I knew it was temporary, but he just ended it and let me know later," she said, filling Hannah in on the gruesome details of that morning's conversation.

"Jerk."

"It's complicated for him, I know, but I can't believe he actually thought I would be so naive," she said, and told Hannah about the phone call she heard and their resulting argument.

Hannah looked thoughtful for a moment. "My Aunt had PTS after a bad car accident—she couldn't even ride in a car for a long time, let alone drive, and it can make people act very strangely, but it sounds more like Reece's ego is just too big for his body, nice as that body is. You have to watch out for yourself, too. You were just trying to help," Hannah said, giving her a hug.

"Yes, that's exactly it! He knows all about my life, he helped me with recovering from the fire, he has been there for me every step of the way, which was just… incredible," Abby said, swiping a hand at a tear that snuck out.

"But then, when I reach out to him, when I want to help, he swatted me back. Told me not to mistake sex for the right to care about him, basically," she concluded with a sniff.

"Ouch."

"Yeah."

"Well, maybe in some ass-backward male way he's trying to protect you by pushing you away," Hannah offered, shrugging.

"Yeah, maybe, but it's stupid."

"Well, he's a *guy,*" Hannah said, and for the first time in hours Abby had reason to laugh.

"I guess. A lesson learned, I suppose."

"And you had some great sex, got to live out a high-school fantasy and got back in the game."

"I would hardly call it getting back in the game," Abby said. "Probably heading for another long dry spell."

They both looked over at the people happily decorating trees. She envied their simple holiday cheer.

"Oh, I don't know. I think you might be putting out the sex vibe."

"The *what?*"

Hannah grinned. "The sex vibe. It's probably pheromones or something, but when someone is sexually active, it's like they put out a signal and attract other people who are interested, too."

"Hannah, what the heck are you talking about? Give me that wine, you've had too much," Abby said, laughing.

"See for yourself," Hannah said, holding her glass

back where Abby couldn't reach it. "A totally hot guy has been checking you out all day."

Abby had no idea what Hannah was talking about until she spotted two cute guys standing by the far edge of the crowd of half-decorated Christmas trees. One smiled at her boldly.

"Where did they come from?" Abby asked Hannah.

"They've been here the whole time, and that one hasn't been able to take his eyes off you, though you've been too distracted to notice. Good thing you have me watching out for you," Hannah said, smiling and waving back at the cute guy.

"Hannah, *don't,*" Abby insisted, but then saw he was already on his way over.

"Why not? It's the perfect distraction from your troubles. Maybe his friend would be interested in doubling," Hannah said, elbowing her slightly.

Abby sent her a look that promised retribution later on, but turned to the handsome guy—whose name was Derek—and offered him a taste of the Baco.

She maintained her professional composure for the first few minutes, but Hannah was right. Derek was charming and obviously interested. Unfortunately for Hannah, his friend was already making a move on another of the event guests, and her friend winked at her, giving her an "oh well" shrug before leaving Abby alone with Derek.

He was a local business owner, too, running his own computer software shop. He was also about three years her junior, but that didn't seem to bother him any. Maybe it shouldn't bother her, either.

He *was* hot, with wavy blond hair and mischievous blue eyes, and he looked great in his jeans, but Abby didn't feel any sparks at all. For all the attraction she felt, Derek could have been her brother.

But she chatted with him, enjoying the distraction from thinking about Reece.

"I'm glad we decided to stop when we saw all the commotion," Derek said, studying the group decorating trees and stepping back to watch Abby fill tasting cups or dole out hot cocoa as people approached the booth.

"I'm glad you're enjoying yourself," she said diplomatically, wondering if there was a way to discourage him without losing a new customer or being rude. He was a nice guy, but contrary to Hannah's theories about sex vibes, Abby wasn't feeling too flirty or sexy at the moment.

"I am. I've never really been into wines. I mostly like a beer after work," he said, smiling at her in that way that surely sent many a girl into a flutter.

"I like beer, too. Many of the gourmet ones are so interesting," she responded vaguely, and that set them off talking about breweries and beer tasting, which she had to admit, was very interesting. He didn't know much about wine, but he was very knowledgeable about beer.

"It looks like the trees are almost done—I'm going to have to do some judging and hand out prizes," she said, hoping to find her exit that way.

Where had Hannah gone?

"Do you need any help?" Derek offered.

Abby was about to refuse, but then she saw Reece,

walking from the barn up to the house. He stood by the front and watched her, not moving.

She felt her annoyance kick in again and smiled brightly at Derek. "Sure. You can help me collect votes," she said, standing close to him as she explained the voting process.

Abby didn't look back, but she heard the door slam in the background and grinned.

Derek was lit up like one of the Christmas trees by her interest, and she had to stop and think while he helped her collect votes for the best tree.

What was she doing? Derek was a sweet guy, as far as she could tell, and she had absolutely no romantic interest in him at all—using him to poke at Reece was ridiculous. She just hadn't been able to help herself. Still, it wasn't fair to Derek.

She watched her new friend smiling with a group of kids as he collected their votes and laughed as he took a snowball to the shoulder from one boy. Abby smiled, wishing she could just flip her emotions off from Reece and on to Derek. But she couldn't.

"You two seemed chummy," Hannah said, appearing back at her side suddenly.

"Where were you?"

"I had to watch over the snowman-making contest," she said innocently.

"Judy is doing that," Abby said knowingly. "You left me alone with him here on purpose."

Hannah grinned. "Did he ask you out?"

"Not yet."

"You going to go?"

"I don't know."

"Then my evil plan worked."

"Reece saw us," Abby said.

Hannah smiled. "I saw him staring at something, and he nearly broke the window in the door when he went inside."

Abby shook her head. "Yeah, I think I got a little carried away and made it look like I was more interested in Derek than I am," she confessed.

Hannah grinned more widely. "Then I would say my evil plan *really* worked. Reece was fit to be tied. Only one thing would get him that worked up at seeing you with another guy."

Hope leapt in Abby's chest, but she squashed it.

"I'm not going to count on that. Nothing has changed."

Derek walked back over, and they wrapped up the contest, awarded the prizes and made sure everyone had a little something to take home with them.

It was a very successful event, in spite of her own personal challenges, and Abby felt good about pulling it off.

When Derek asked her out before he was leaving, she regretfully declined, leaving Hannah shaking her head. Derek smiled and gave her his email, just in case, writing it down on a napkin and sticking it in her pocket.

"Why couldn't I have met him a few weeks ago?" she asked Hannah as the yard turned dark, and she sat with her friend on the porch step, looking at a field filled with brightly decorated trees and a crowd of snowmen. If she had met Derek then, maybe none of this would have happened.

"Would that have made a difference, really?"

Abby sighed. "Probably not."

Whatever was between her and Reece, if anything, it wasn't easy, and it wasn't what she'd counted on. Still, she knew she wouldn't trade one second of the fun or passion they'd had, even though it blew up in her face.

"Want to spend the night at my place?" Hannah offered.

Abby shook her head. Even though it was awkward, she and Reece were in this until the end, and she'd handle it. She wasn't sure how, but she didn't really have any other choice.

9

REECE'S HANDS OPENED and closed around the leather-covered wheel. His old friend Brody Palmer, who was sitting in the passenger's seat, chuckled. Brody had come up from Florida to see family for a few days, and Reece had really enjoyed a night out with a friend, having a few beers and talking shop. It was also the first time he'd driven anything other than his dad's old, slow truck for a while, and truth be told, he didn't drive that if he could avoid it, relying on friends or public transport.

It felt good, though he was somewhat nervous. That was to be expected, right? His mind went to Abby, distracting him from his doubts. It had been a week since their argument, and they managed to move around each other without a lot of fuss, talking when they had to, but not much else. He also seen her talking with the fire investigator sent to do the second report, and the strain she'd been under was obvious. He made himself scarce, not wanting to add to it. How could they think she would have torched her own place?

He wondered where she went when she was out.

With the young stud he'd seen her flirting with at the Christmas tree contest?

He'd wanted to punch the guy in the face, but that wasn't his right. Never was. Still, it had been all he could do to keep from crossing the field and claiming Abby as his.

Which left him more confused than ever.

"Stop feeling her up and drive already," Brody said, making Reece laugh.

"Sorry. It's been a while," he said, enjoying the snug fit of the seat and the powerful purr of the engine as he hit the gas and pulled out from the restaurant where he'd met Brody for dinner. Brody had been in the NASCAR circuit for a while and was thinking about retiring, which he'd told Reece over dinner.

"It's like sex. You might be a little rusty, but it will come back to you," Brody reassured.

"You sure you trust me not to scratch her?" he asked with a hint of humor, but his nerves betrayed him.

Brody's new Dodge Charger SRT8 was a nice machine. This was the most car he'd driven since he crashed, and his hands were a bit sweaty, his heart slamming not from excitement, but apprehension.

"It's right to be nervous after a crash," Brody said, reading him. "It's normal, but if you want back in, you have to start working through it. Open her up gradually. See how it feels. You can back off if you need to."

His friend's understanding helped ease his anxiety. Brody was absolutely right—how could Reece expect to return to driving if he couldn't drive a regular road car?

He left the parking lot, and relaxed as the car started moving.

This was familiar. It felt good.

As they hit the lake road heading to the winery, Reece picked up speed, feeling his reflexes kick in, and he laughed with pure pleasure.

"Told you," Brody said, chuckling, too.

Except for when he'd been making love to Abby, he hadn't been this pumped in some time. Her face, her scent, came back to him with startling clarity, and he lost track of what he was doing for a moment, which had him backing off on the gas.

"You okay?" Brody asked.

"Yeah, sorry. I was distracted for a minute," he said, irritated. He still craved her touch, but he couldn't afford any distractions if he was going to drive, and that included women. Even Abby.

Reece focused for the rest of the drive up the side of the lake, turning into the driveway where he found a crowd of cars in the parking lot.

"I guess the party is still going, but we can head into the house, have a few beers," he said to Brody, parking the Charger and handing his buddy the keys. "Thanks for that. It felt good."

Brody stuck the keys in the pocket of the leather bomber jacket he wore, watching Reece speculatively. "I heard they were thinking of a new guy for your team," he said.

"Yeah, I heard that, too. Hope to convince them differently, but it's hard, being stuck here."

"I know a few guys at Daytona. If you want to fly in for a day, I could set up a test drive for you. We could go down there for a few times around the track, do some timed runs, if you want to see how it goes."

Reece knew he should jump at the opportunity, but the sweat broke out on his hands again. He didn't understand why he was reacting this way, and it pissed him off.

"Sure, set it up," he said evenly, though his stomach lurched as they walked up to the house.

His left leg was still bothering him. He was starting to think it might never get better, though he knew it felt worse after being locked into position while driving. Exercise and time would solve that problem, he kept telling himself.

"So what's the big event?" Brody asked, nodding toward the group of cars.

"Bachelorette party," Reece said with a laugh, shaking his head.

"Are you kidding me?"

"Nope."

Reece explained about Abby, and how she was working out of the winery. The bachelor party was at a bar in town, but Sandra had decided to have her party at the winery. Reece had overheard that conversation on his way through the house one day.

Brody stopped, rubbing his chin with his thumb and forefinger, grinning as he looked toward the reception rooms. "Should we crash?"

Reece laughed. "We're not eighteen anymore."

His friend cocked an eyebrow in his direction. "Yeah, we wouldn't have known what to do with a roomful of half-drunk chicks in the mood to party when we were eighteen," he said, making Reece laugh harder, his former tension dissolving.

"And you do now?" Reece teased back, slapping

Brody on the shoulder, but Brody was already heading toward the party. Reece followed, reluctantly.

"It's kind of Abby's thing," he hedged. "Maybe we should just stick to the house."

"Gotta get your spirit of adventure back, friend," Brody said with a grin, and Reece gave in and continued to follow. They made their way over to the tasting room, walking in the side door where it was dark in the lobby, moving like spies along the bar and cracking open the door to the reception room out back.

Reece wasn't sure what he expected to see, but it sure wasn't what he saw.

"You sure this is the *bachelorette* party?" Brody asked on a whisper, his eyes wide.

"Yeah," he answered, though he had to admit to a moment of confusion, as well.

At the far side of the room, women all gathered, and Reece had to blink a few times to believe what he was seeing. Abby had been very hush-hush about the party and changed the subject or was vague when he asked how it was going. Now he knew why.

He'd figured the party would either be a bunch of women dancing or talking, or sticking dollar bills in some young guy's jock strap, but instead, a ministage had been set up on the far end of the room, and there was a pole that braced from ceiling to floor.

And the women were taking turns dancing around it. They had their clothes on, of course. And most of them collapsed laughing as they tried to imitate classic stripper moves—some more successful than others—to songs playing so loudly all he could hear was music and shrieks of laughter, along with encouraging comments.

"Women are strange," Brody said. "Don't they usually get mad at us for going to watch this kind of thing?"

Reece laughed, edging the door open for a better view of the merriment. It was all innocent fun and games, and no one even noticed they were there, they were all enjoying themselves so much.

He naturally sought out Abby, who was standing to the side, monitoring the event and making sure all was going well. She smiled and spoke to Hannah, who stood by her side, the two women standing apart from the main action.

The song ended and Sandra, much happier than the day he'd found her screaming at Abby out in the field, took the stage. She definitely appeared to be tilting a bit, a martini sloshing dangerously in her hand.

She took a microphone and grinned at the group of women in front of her.

"This is such a blast—as you know, it's all on video, and I'll be sure to let you know which cuts make it to YouTube tomorrow," she promised. Laughter and a few playful threats ensued.

"But the martinis aren't gone and we're not done yet!" she announced to a chorus of hooting and howling.

"And not everyone has taken their turn, and we said everyone has to take a turn," she warned, turning to face Abby, who was still talking to Hannah.

The crowd cheered again as Sandra said, "Now we know Abby Harper can throw a monster bachelorette party, but can she dance?"

Abby stopped midconversation with Hannah, just then noticing the room's attention was on her. Her eyes widened and she shook her head.

"Oh, this just got interesting," Brody said, leering at Abby and Hannah. Reece elbowed him.

"The one on the right is Abby," Reece told him, but the light warning in his voice was clear.

Brody grinned. "So the one on the left is free?"

Brody was a shameless womanizer, teased in the media as to whether he had more trophies or romantic conquests. About the only thing in life he was serious about was his driving. Behind the wheel, he was all business, but out in the world, he was all play.

"Yeah, bud, go for it," Reece said, thinking it might be funny to see Brody get shot down. He'd known Hannah as long as he'd known Abby, and Hannah was as no-nonsense as they came, and she didn't suffer fools.

Abby was still vociferously protesting, even as Sandra tugged her up on stage, everyone laughing and daring her to do it.

When Abby was left alone by the pole, the crowd clapping to the beat of some bump-and-grind rock song that started playing, Abby laughed, put a hand to her face in embarrassment and rolled her eyes.

"Oh, my God, she's going to do it," Reece said, finding himself inexplicably breathless.

Abby was dressed in a very simple black dress that seemed conservative next to some of the outfits in the room, but when she kicked her heels off and grabbed the pole, Reece's cock jerked and hardened.

She slid her back up and down the pole, the simple dress sliding down off her shoulder slightly, and rising as she bent her knee to reveal a smooth expanse of thigh. When her head fell back in apparent sexual bliss, Reece heard Brody hiss a breath and elbowed him again.

When she came back up, vamping for the girls, she looked across the room and froze as she saw him.

He smiled, nodding once, and mischief sparkled in her expression. No one seemed to notice them watching but her.

Her eyes stayed on his as she started dancing again. Wrapping herself around that pole like a pro, she bent forward to show the tops of beautiful breasts as she shimmied, impressing him with flexibility that he knew he wanted to learn more about.

"*That's* your high school girlfriend?" Brody said in awe.

"No, she was just a neighbor then, a girl I knew," Reece said, not looking away.

"And now?"

"Not sure," Reece said, wanting to stop talking and focus.

Laughing, Abby held her hand out. All hell broke loose when Hannah strutted up on stage, wearing a classic wool skirt and plain white blouse, but Reece suddenly saw the smart-mouthed accountant that he knew turn into a sexy vixen. She undid a few buttons and her hair swished around her face, making those dark-rimmed glasses downright intriguing.

Brody lost all control and started whistling, catcalling for more, and the women turned, gaping, a moment of silence falling over the room, except for the heavy beat of the music still playing.

Reece wasn't sure what their reception would be, but he was poised to either apologize or make a run for it.

Brody's eyes were glued to Hannah, and he seemed to care less if they had been discovered, yelling to the women to start dancing again.

Laughter broke out, and some women came back, taking Reece and Brody by the hands, pulling them forward and insisting if they wanted to join the party, that *they* had to dance.

Reece laughed, but "over my dead body" was his silent reply to that. Brody, though, was in party form, grabbing a martini and jumping up on stage with a shocked Hannah, leading her to dance more with him, just as Reece took Abby's hand and helped her down.

"I missed you" was the first thing he said, and he realized it was true.

"I missed you, too," she admitted.

His eyes devoured her flushed cheeks and the rest of the room around them fell away.

"I don't get the dancing thing, but I sure did like it," he said in a low voice.

She grinned. "I don't know, either. It's some stripper fantasy, girl-power deal, I guess," she said, shrugging. "It was fun, though."

They both cracked up when they looked back to see Brody dancing around the pole.

Something clicked for Reece when he heard Abby laugh. He wanted to drag her off to a dark corner and take her now.

She seemed to know what he was thinking. The party had taken on a life of its own, and no one even noticed them anymore.

Before she could find some reason to change her mind, he took her by the hand and led her out of the room, into the tasting room, behind the bar. It was mostly dark, and no one else was there, though everyone was about twenty feet away at the party.

He backed her up against the wall, silencing anything she might say with a kiss that made his need clear. She moaned into his mouth, and as he slipped his hand up under the skirt of her dress, he found her slick, as aroused as he was.

"It's not the hedges, but it will do," he said roughly into her neck, need clawing at him as he picked up the scent of her sweat and sex, her skin hot from dancing and arousal.

"Someone might come out, they could see," she said, but he knew from her tone it was exciting her more… and she didn't ask him to stop.

"Yeah, they could, so we'd better hurry," he agreed, freeing his erection from his jeans and lifting her hips, cradling her butt in his hands so that she could wrap her legs around him.

Reece wasted no time getting inside of her, pushing deep and hard, taking her in short, quick thrusts that made her arch against him. She muffled a cry of pleasure as she dug her fingers into his shoulders, hanging on. She was hot and tight around him, and he didn't care if someone did come out and catch them, he needed her too much.

He didn't think he'd ever been this aroused. He was starving for her. In fact, he never would have risked this kind of public exposure given his responsibilities to the team and his sponsors, but right now, he didn't have to worry about that.

He leaned down, bracing Abby against the wall so that he could suck a nipple through the fabric of her dress. That sent her over the edge. She sank her teeth into his shoulder as she came, holding on tight and trying to hold back the scream that became a low keening against his neck.

He couldn't stop, either, and found her mouth, plundering it with a deep kiss as he exploded inside of her, the orgasm making his legs weak, but he rode it out, taking every last bit of pleasure she offered him.

When the moment passed, they were both sweaty, sticky and breathless. Reece heard voices coming toward them and they quickly ducked down behind the bar. Abby was illuminated in a sliver of light that angled down from the front windows, her eyes wide and sparkling, hair tousled. She covered her mouth to smother a giggle.

He pulled her in close, wrapping his arms around her as the voices came closer.

It was Brody and—if he was correct—Hannah.

He felt Abby shift in his arms, she must have realized, too, and reached to see. He held her still, putting a finger to her lips until their friends moved on, and Reece heard the grumbling engine of the Charger rev to life.

"Sounds like Hannah is taking home a little Christmas cheer," Abby said, chuckling, and Reece grinned as they both stood up, surveying the area as they fixed their clothes and emerged into the other room.

"Who was that, anyway?" she asked, threading fingers through her hair to smooth it down.

He ran his eyes over her and wanted to mess it right back up again.

"My friend Brody. Palmer," he added.

"Like, *the* Brody Palmer?" she asked. "Are you telling me my best friend just left with *Brody Palmer?* The one whose fan site has a poll keeping track of whether he's ridden more cars or women?"

Reece winced and opted for being straightforward.

"Yeah, that would be the one."

Abby groaned. "I don't know whether I should call her to warn her off or congratulate her," she said.

"You can't believe everything you hear in the media," Reece said, chuckling.

Abby eyed him doubtfully, and he caved.

"Well, okay, when it comes to Brody, most of that is kind of true, but he's a good guy, I promise. She'll be okay with him," he insisted.

"If you say so," she commented, smiling, and pressed in close. She kept Hannah's comments about wishing she could find a hot guy to use for sex to herself. It looked like her friend's wish had come true.

"How about you?"

"What?" he asked, playing dumb.

"More cars or women?" she asked with a grin.

"I don't have anyone running polls, but I'm pretty sure I can say cars," he answered, nuzzling her neck. "I'm not a saint, but I'm no Brody Palmer."

"Thank heavens," she said, laughing and wrapping her arms around his neck, sighing.

Bright lights flicked on and they flew apart to find a grinning, soused bride-to-be facing them. Sandra stared at them for a minute, still smiling.

"Sandra, are you okay?"

"I'm *won-fer-dul*," she said, lurching forward to wrap her arms around Abby in a drunken hug. Abby sagged under the slack weight of the woman, who mumbled praise about the best party ever and being so sorry she had threatened to "shoe" Abby after the fire.

"It's okay, Sandra. I knew you were just upset, and wouldn't really sue me," Abby comforted, trying to support her weight and looking over Sandra's shoulder for help.

Reece came to her rescue, slinging one of Sandra's arms over his shoulder, bracing most of the weight as they got her to one of the fireplace chairs and gently deposited her in it.

"What are you doing with the not-so-blushing bride?" he asked with a grin.

Abby sighed. "I can find out which of her friends or sisters is most sober, and see if they can get her upstairs to her room. I have all of their car keys over at the house, so no one is going anywhere tonight. Big sleepover," she said, chuckling, and Reece relaxed. "They have a group brunch planned for tomorrow morning, so once I get them set tonight, I'm done."

"What can I do to help?" he asked, and she looked at him in surprise.

"You can't take care of all of this alone, and Hannah is gone for the night," Reece pointed out.

"You're sure?" she said, and he saw the doubt in her eyes. He didn't blame her.

But now that he'd had her in his arms again, he knew that he didn't want to let her go one minute sooner than he had to.

"Absolutely. Abby, I'm sorry I was an ass last week. I guess I thought it would be easier if I put some distance between us, but it wasn't."

"Reece," she said on a sigh, leaning her forehead against him.

"That guy, at the Christmas tree event…did you go out with him?"

God, he felt sixteen, but he had to know.

"No. I was just trying to tick you off."

"It worked," he said with a grin, but then became serious again. "I didn't mean to hurt you. I just…I don't know," he admitted, feeling foolish. "I was messed up."

She pressed a kiss to the corner of his lips. "I know. Me, too."

Suddenly the world seemed a little more right again, and Reece blew out a breath, looking at his watch.

"You can go see what's what. I can start cleaning up, if you want," he said.

"Thanks. I appreciate it. I'll be right back."

He watched her walk away, all female grace and strength, and knew he couldn't fight what he felt for her anymore, but he had no idea where it was heading, either. Nothing had changed—and everything had changed.

"Abby?" he called out, before she disappeared back into the reception room.

She turned. "Hmm?"

"Maybe we should leave that pole up, though, just for a night or two," he said, imagining he'd like a show for one.

The sexy, mischievous look in her eyes as she smiled told him she agreed.

10

ABBY WAS GETTING USED to her life on a roller coaster, and when it meant she was able to wake up in Reece's bed, that was definitely okay with her.

She wasn't interested in fighting it anymore, releasing all the doubt and worry. They were good together. She wanted him, and apparently he wanted her. She shivered, thinking about the wonderful, desperate way he'd taken her the night before, standing up, behind the wine bar. The sex had been fast, a little awkward and... spectacular.

They'd worked side-by-side the rest of the evening, some understanding hammered out even though they didn't talk very much at all.

As much as she wanted him again, they'd both crashed as soon as they hit the mattress, exhausted and wrapped around each other. She remembered feeling a deep satisfaction that he seemed to have missed her as much as she missed him.

Maybe that was foolish, but she didn't care.

She stared at the empty pillow beside her—he'd probably gotten up early to work out. Her cell phone rang, interrupting her thoughts. Hannah.

"Hey," Abby said cheerfully. "I didn't expect to hear from you today, you wild woman," she teased her friend.

"You know me, I'm an early bird," Hannah said, her voice practically singing with I-had-a-night-of-wild-sex energy. "Even when I was up very, very late."

"Do tell."

"Later, promise. Right now, we were wondering if you'd be interested in brunch."

"We?"

"Brody and I. We're calling for both of you, but if you want, you could just come yourself."

Abby detected the unspoken question in Hannah's voice—she must have seen them leave together, and wondered what had happened.

"I'm sure Reece will want to come, too."

Hannah laughed knowingly. "So your cold spell is over," she said happily.

"Most definitely," Abby said with a smile. "Where should we meet you?"

They named a time and place, and Abby got up, taking off what little she had on and padding to the bathroom, where she had just heard the water turn on. Losing her robe, she smiled, pulling the door open to find Reece waiting.

"I was hoping the noise might wake you up," he said with an unabashed grin, holding out a hand to her.

"Wow," she said, not hiding her awe. He was using the master bath, and she had been using the guest bath attached to her room. Hers was very nice, she had no complaints, but this was just…sinful.

The entire space was composed of granite with specks of gold, black and dark red lending a warm touch, textured on the floor so as to avoid being slippery, and smooth, but with a matte finish, on the sides. Plants lined a window that set a few feet above them, draping down, obviously loving the high humidity and light. Abby felt like she was stepping into a hidden cave with a waterfall.

There were five jets at different heights, and a bench seat that ran almost the entire length of the shower, with a shelf of soaps, shampoos, body oils, sponges, loofahs and pretty much anything else you could think of. You could even adjust the lighting, bright or soft, and the controls for the water temperature were digital so you could set the degree—no guessing.

"This isn't a shower. This is shower heaven," she said.

"Yeah, it's extreme. My dad always called it 'The Lagoon,'" he said with a laugh.

"That's it exactly."

"It was my mom's pet project. She set out to create the perfect bathroom one year. It actually was featured in a home décor magazine. She was on top of the world."

"She nailed it," Abby agreed breathlessly, and he laughed as she went into his arms under the hot spray.

His hands covered and massaged her breasts as they kissed, and he added, "Now *this* is shower heaven."

"Mmm-hmm," she agreed, her hands dipping low to stroke his ready erection, making him groan. She was intrigued when he trembled as she reached lower, stroking a finger over his balls and petting the soft skin deep between his thighs.

"Come here," he said as he sat on the bench and pulled her on to his lap, angled slightly so she could kiss him as the water poured over them from seemingly everywhere.

She started to turn to face him, to straddle him, but he shook his head. "You'll punish your knees on the stone. Like this," he said, stretching out his legs straight and moving her over him.

"Oh...*oh*," she gasped as he slid deep inside.

He held her there against him, kissing her ears, her neck. His hands covered her breasts, plucking and rolling hard, wet nipples between his fingers until she was writhing.

She had a feeling he'd planned that, and she liked a man who thought ahead. The throbbing of the hot water against her flesh and the sensation of him buried deep inside had her moaning as an easy orgasm rolled over her. Reece whispered hot, raw things in her ear as she came, and then came again.

Breathless and panting, she pushed forward, still poised against him, bracing her hands on his knees, looking back with a sexy wink.

"I like this," she said, enjoying how his hands covered her bottom, his fingers digging in a little as he brought her down the way that he needed.

"Me, too."

She moved her right hand from his knee to stroke herself as she took him deep and ground against him in a way that had him yelling her name, arching up and pushing even deeper as they came together.

She relaxed back against him, turning her face into the strong column of his neck.

"That was so good. It's always good with you," she said, wrapping her fingers in his as the water washed over them.

"I'm glad you think so."

"I do."

He helped her up and stood with her, grabbing a soft natural sponge and some soap. He washed her carefully, tenderly, and she nearly purred. She'd never felt this cared for, and the intimacy was stunning as he bent before her, washing her legs and between them, planting kisses where the shower washed away the soap. She was feeling sparks again before he was back at eye level.

"Do you like games, Abby?"

A flicker of anticipation teased her.

"Like Monopoly?" she asked innocently.

He smiled, and pulled her closer, whispering in her ear. Her breath hitched. How was it that her fantasies seemed to be his?

"I love those kinds of games," she said, finding it hard to breathe.

"Come here then," he said, pulling her upright.

He positioned her by the edge of the spray, and she looked up, seeing the two ties that hung limply from the shower rod. Realization dawned.

"Oh. I thought you had just left your laundry in here," she said, her heart stuttering as he lifted her arm and pulled one tie down to her wrist.

"Make sure the ties won't give," she said, daringly, and saw his eyes darken as they met hers.

"Is this comfortable?" he asked, securing the tie.

She wiggled her fingers, and pulled. The knots were solid. A slight edge of apprehension rose, but curiosity and excitement outweighed it.

"I'm good," she said, watching him step back and look at her.

"We're going to do what I told you, and you're okay with it? My rules?"

"Yes," she said, as submissively as she could.

"Good," he said, his eyes dark and passionate on hers as he stroked himself to semihardness.

She watched, fascinated, unable to take her eyes away from him. She'd never watched a man pleasure himself, and felt herself get wet from more than the shower.

"You'd like to watch me finish this, wouldn't you?"

She struggled, flexing her fingers, wanting to touch, to go to him, but he was out of reach. And if she couldn't touch him, she wanted to touch herself, suddenly craving release again.

"I'd like that very much," she admitted. "But there's a problem."

"What?"

"I want to come again, too."

"Well," he said, teasingly, softly, "we'll both get there, eventually."

She frowned. "Eventually?"

He walked over to her, leaning in to nuzzle her neck, and she whimpered, needing the touch.

"You'll see."

He kissed her sweetly, then moved down her body in a string of butterfly kisses, leaving sparks of heat everywhere, but not giving her anything near what she needed. He brushed his thumbs and then his lips over her nipples, lightly, teasing some more, until she was almost limp and begging.

Then he went down farther, and she braced for his kiss between her legs, but he only ran his hands up and down her legs, kissing and nibbling at the insides of her thighs. She opened herself as much as she could, trying to show him what she needed.

"You want my mouth on you, Abby?"

"Please, yes," she said weakly. Desire was a hot weight in her abdomen, a bomb needing to explode.

He nodded and whispered, "Okay," against her skin, then used both hands to spread her slick flesh, but rather than planting his mouth against her, he flicked his tongue against her clit, the sensations intense but fleeting, not constant enough to push her over. She tried to press against him, to find the pressure she needed to come, but he would move and she cried out in lust and need.

"Please, Reece. I don't think I want to play anymore," she said.

He stood, his jaw tight, his eyes dark. "Abby, I'm hard as rock, ready to explode—again. I haven't felt need like this in years. I want to pull you up and fuck you until we both dissolve under the water," he said, and his raw language only excited her more.

"Do it," she urged, wanting exactly that. "Just think how good it would be, Reece. You could take me any way you want…and I want you to," she tempted, trying to break him. "Whatever you want, however you want me," she whispered.

By the look on his face and the way his cock jerked at her words, it was working.

He came up close to her, and she cheered inside her mind, celebrating her win.

He smiled and then did something she never expected, bringing his hand down on her bottom in a stinging swat. "Stop that. We both have to wait. Those are the rules."

The sting from the swat turned to heat on her skin, and she found she craved more, anything that would relieve the torturous pressure of arousal inside of her. They'd just made love minutes before, but it had been too long, and her body was on fire for more.

He rubbed his hand over the spot where he had spanked her, and brushed his lips against hers, then kissed her more deeply.

Their bodies were hardly touching, though their mouths tried to make up for it, mating furiously.

"Reece, I need you," she said, breaking the kiss to breathe.

"I need you, too, Abby," he said roughly. "So much."

He reached up past her, the length of his body touching hers, making her shudder, and she heard a noise. One arm fell free, then the other.

She looked down at her wrists, and he reached over to shut off the water.

She stared at him, stunned. "You really mean it, don't you? You're going to make us both wait?"

He nodded, stepping away and coming back with a heated towel that he wrapped around her. She was dizzy with arousal, and he pulled her up close, rubbing her back soothingly.

"That's right. That's the game."

"What if I don't want to wait?"

"You already agreed to play," he said, pulling her

behind him and grabbing a towel for himself. "Don't worry. I'm just as hot as you are, and you'll have your turn later," he promised. "Didn't you say we have to go meet Brody and Hannah for breakfast."

She almost groaned in dismay. She'd almost forgotten. How was she going to get through brunch with friends, as wound up as she was? She couldn't even think straight, she was so turned on.

It was wonderful.

She was tuned into him more closely than she had ever been to anything in her life, as if she was aware of every movement, every breath. She rubbed her wrists.

"You okay?" he asked, clearly concerned.

"Yes. I liked how it felt. I wanted it to last longer," she admitted, starting to calm down a little. She was on edge, certain that so much as a touch from him might send her into climax, but now…now she also wanted to see how long they could last. How crazy they could make each other before they gave in.

And she was very much looking forward to her turn to push Reece to his limit.

He smiled at her, as if he'd read every thought. It was incredibly intimate, linking them together in a way she hadn't experienced with anyone else, ever.

As they got dressed, he leaned in and planted a kiss on her lips, whispering, "It's going to be worth every second we wait, I promise," he said.

She believed it.

REECE SHIFTED IN HIS chair at the table, dealing with an on-and-off hard-on all through brunch. Abby was a clever lover—and a little mean—he thought with a smile.

When he'd told her he wanted to tie her up and tease her until she begged, she'd been all for it. When he told her he was going to leave them both on edge, not give in, she'd doubted him, but it was perfect. The constant potential for satisfaction—or not—was like live electricity crackling between them.

He'd read about extended sexual seduction practices. They included but also went beyond Tantra to create arousal that lasted for days, resulting in climax for both partners that was off the scale—but he'd never been with anyone he desired enough to actually try it. He imagined him and Abby seducing each other with baths, massages, meals and light sexual teasing for days before having sex. He'd always wondered what that would be like.

Now he knew.

She became adept at the game very quickly.

Small touches to his knee or his thigh were bad enough, but the way she innocently worked bondage references into her conversation taunted him, reminding him of how incredibly erotic she had looked hours ago, and how close he had come to taking her again.

But this was better. The play was demonical, but fun.

His focus was on her hand as she appeared to absently rub her wrist as they ate and chatted—not because it hurt, but because she knew, the little minx, that it would be driving him out of his mind to think about tying her up again. The first time had been an experiment, and way too brief.

"So anyway," Brody said, stretching back in his chair,

grinning and eyeing Reece speculatively as Brody's hand landed on Hannah's nape.

It was an oddly possessive gesture, Reece thought. He'd been surprised enough that Brody was at a brunch with a woman he slept with. It might be a first. Reece certainly didn't know the details of Brody's love life, except that most of his stories of the women he met included a hasty exit before morning light.

Hannah seemed quite happy with herself this morning, too. Interesting.

"Anyway," Brody started again, "I talked with a friend down at Daytona this morning. If you're interested, we could fly there later today, do a test run tomorrow, see how it feels, get your legs back under you," Brody announced.

Reece hadn't seen that coming, either. Brody was full of surprises. He knew he'd told him to set it up, but he thought it would probably be weeks, not hours.

"Wow, that was fast," was all he could say.

"Strike while the iron is hot," Brody said, chugging back his orange juice. "We'd have to leave later today, but I can get us down there. Friend of mine has a private plane and pilot here that he's willing to loan out."

Reece was dumbstruck, and he knew his response should have been immediate. Brody's eyes narrowed as he watched him, but he didn't say anything else.

Reece was dealing with the fact that his first response had not been *hell, yeah,* but that he didn't want to leave Abby, not when they had just found their footing again.

Which was ridiculous. He'd be back after a day or so. She'd still be here, right?

"Reece, you have to get back behind the wheel before they're even going to look at you for the new season. You have to get your mojo," Brody added.

Reece knew he shouldn't need arm-twisting, and jumped when he felt Abby's hand cover his in a visible show of support.

"You should go," she said, her voice sure.

He looked at her and she didn't waver, just gave him a single nod before squeezing his hand and returning to her breakfast.

He wasn't sure how to respond to that, either—was she able to let him go so easily? Why did that bother him? He'd done nothing but tell her that he was leaving since they first met.

"You should come with me," he said to her, the words leaving his lips almost before the idea had fully formed in his brain. It made sense though. For one thing, he felt better when he had Abby with him—he'd slept peacefully for the first time last night, and his legs or arm weren't bothering him at all this morning.

Maybe it was the sex, the release, the stimulation or just her personal magic, but she made him feel good. And he needed to feel good if he was going to get into a car and hit a track at one-eighty plus for the first time in months.

"Oh, I don't know...." she said, frowning. "The wedding is only ten days off—"

"You have most of that prepped," Hannah interrupted. "Anything else is up to the families, except for the decorating, but you don't need to do that now. I checked the schedule, and the next thing you have is the Christmas and Chocolate party this Friday night. You can manage to take a few days off. C'mon Abby, let's take a little vacation," Hannah urged.

"You're both going?" Reece asked, looking at Brody with even more surprise.

"Yeah. Hannah says she wants some excitement, and I can't think of anything more exciting than being at the track. So she's coming with me for a month of preseason."

Abby and Reece were both struck silent with surprise. Hannah's cheeks were warm, but her eyes were bright with pure joy.

"I hope that's okay, Abby, I was going to talk to you before Brody decided to just leap in and volunteer the information," she said, sliding him an affectionate look. "But January is always slow, and you can take my apartment while you're working on getting things done with the winery, I mean, you know, if you're still not at Reece's after the New Year," Hannah said.

Abby nodded, and didn't appear to know what to say. Reece put his hand on hers this time and squeezed, turning to her so that they were only looking at each other.

"I'd really like it if you could come with me," he said. "It would mean a lot, but I also understand if you can't."

Abby, looking slightly cornered, shook her head, as if trying to clear her thoughts. She turned her hand over to hold Reece's, an encouraging sign.

"Hannah is right. I can close for a few days, not much happening on weekdays now anyway. I'll have Judy come by to look in on the horses and animals. She's done that for me before," she said.

"So you'll come?" Reece asked, feeling far too hopeful.

She paused for another moment, then smiled. "Yes, it'll be fun," she replied. "And I want to be there for you."

"Great! I'll make the flight arrangements right now," Brody, their man of action, said, planting a quick kiss on Hannah's mouth. He pulled his cell phone from his pocket and stood up from the table.

Reece leaned in to kiss Abby's cheek. "Thank you. This will be a lot less nerve-racking with you there."

She was obviously surprised at his unvarnished admission, and he was, too, but it was the truth. He was developing emotions that amounted to far more than lust for Abby. He had a need for her that went beyond the physical.

She was different than any woman he'd ever known, and he didn't want to lose whatever was growing between them.

What they would do about that, long-term, he had no idea, but for now, he would just take the curves as they came.

Hannah was grinning at them, all dewey-eyed.

"I'm so glad you guys made up," she said.

Reece straightened in his chair, realizing Abby would have, of course, told her about their fight, and no doubt what a jerk he was. But the way she looked right now, happy and hopeful, made him a bit twitchy. He was willing to admit that he had some serious feelings for Abby, but he wasn't entirely comfortable having assumptions made about them as a couple.

"So you're going to hang out with Brody at the track for a month?" he said to Hannah, changing the topic.

"I need some adventure. This sounds…adventurous."

"You follow racing?" Reece asked.

"No, not at all. But I guess I'll learn," she said with a goofy smile, picking apart a croissant.

Reece liked Brody. He was a good friend, and a great driver. But somehow, he felt like he had to say something to Hannah.

"I hope you're not putting too much stock into this, Hannah. Just so you know. He's a good man, but, well, you know what I'm trying to say. I'm surprised he was even here for breakfast," Reece said bluntly, drawing a shocked look from Abby, but Hannah just stared, and then burst out laughing.

"Thanks, Reece, but Brody made it quite clear that he's not interested in anything permanent. That's perfect, because all I want is a month of hot sex and something new in my life before I come back to my routine," she said, making Reece choke on his coffee.

"You two should be perfect together, then," he agreed, laughing.

Abby was uncharacteristically quiet, focused on the remainder of her breakfast, but he could practically hear the wheels spinning in her mind. Right now though, all he cared about was that she would be with him.

They'd have a few days in sunny Florida to go to the track, and to hopefully continue their fun and games.

As much as some excitement had filtered through about the prospect of getting back into a car, it was disconcerting to know that the second item excited him the most.

_11_

ABBY SQUINTED AS SHE DEPLANED, walking down the short course of steps onto the tarmac. She hadn't flown anywhere in quite some time, and never in a private jet. It had been a lot of fun. She'd forgotten how much she enjoyed the speed and thrill of takeoffs, checking out the landscape below as she flew by and the joy of setting feet to ground again. They'd had a smooth flight, and it was only early evening, the weather clear and warm.

She was also starving and, frankly, so horny she could hardly stand it. The close quarters of the plane had given them plenty of time to play their secret game, with quick touches and teasing talk or glances. She figured she might help him relax once they got to their condo, a place Brody owned right by the track.

But there was more than sex going on between them. Reece had thanked her about ten times since brunch, and it warmed her to know that her presence here meant so much to him. She could also detect the fine tension in him. She knew this was a big deal for him, and she was perhaps more nervous for him than he was for himself.

She didn't want to think about where it was all leading. They had something new, some kind of deeper connection, an intimacy that had blossomed quickly and almost without her realizing it. It was as if, after the argument, they had come back together more deeply than before.

Or maybe it was just her. Somehow, regardless of all of the external circumstances and doubts, she knew she could trust Reece, and she wanted to be with him, no matter what the future held.

She was dying to talk to Hannah about her arrangement with Brody, and what had happened to make her friend take off on such a wild lark. She seized the opportunity as they crossed the terminal to a large SUV that was waiting for them. Brody had thought of everything. The men walked ahead, and she slowed down, hanging back with Hannah.

"So…a month with Brody?" she asked, opening the door for Hannah to elaborate.

"Yeah, it's crazy, I know," Hannah said, shaking her head, her strawberry-blond hair swinging over her shoulders. "I wanted to talk to you privately first, since I know this affects you, too, with the winery, but Brody, well, he's kind of a force of nature," she said with a grin.

Abby smiled. "Yeah, that's the perfect description," she agreed. "Must have been some night you had with him, but are you sure a month is going to work out? It's a long time with someone you barely know," Abby said.

"Well, I can always come back early if I don't like it, or if things aren't good. But, Abby, he's amazing. If the month with him is anything like the other night, I'm not sure a month would be enough. I could get addicted."

Abby frowned. "That's another problem altogether. What Reece was talking about. These guys…some of them settle down, but not Reece. Not Brody. I don't want you getting heartbroken," Abby said.

Do as I say, but not as I do, she thought to herself. She wanted to save her friend some pain, if she could.

"I won't. I have no interest in love," Hannah continued. "I just want to be free for a while, to get out of my routine and live a little before I come back and probably end up marrying some nice, safe, dependable man and raising our two-point-eight."

Abby couldn't begrudge her friend that, in fact, she understood all too well. She loved their small-town life on the lake, on the vineyards, but it was a relatively ordinary life. Reece and Brody were extraordinary men.

But it was even more seductive for Hannah, Abby imagined. While she and Reece had grown up on the vineyards with parents who were successful enough to provide some of the extras like college and vacations, Hannah hadn't.

Her parents owned a local farm that had become defunct. Most of Hannah's youth had been beyond difficult, her father working too hard and dying of a heart attack when she was only ten. Her mom had had to work constantly after that to keep the house, and they had eventually sold and lived in an apartment in Ithaca.

Hannah had lost her dad and her home, and yet she'd never moaned and felt sorry for herself, which is something Abby admired so much. Hannah had spent many nights and weekends at Abby's house when they were kids, and she felt more like her sister than her friend.

Hannah's mother did better now, but that was largely

due to Hannah working her way through state college on loans and scholarships, and making life better for both of them.

Abby knew it was no accident that Hannah had studied accounting and that she worked like a dog. Hannah applied the same logic to her love life—she wouldn't marry a man who risked her security. So Abby knew that Brody really was just a wild fling, and if anyone deserved some fun and time away, it was Hannah.

Her friend's sexy brashness made her smile to herself, and she sighed as they were almost to the car.

"Yeah, that's what I thought with Reece at the beginning. Just be careful."

"You two seem more serious now, I take it?" Hannah queried.

"I'm not sure. The other night was...I don't know what it was," she said honestly, with another sigh. "I care about him. I think he cares about me. But as far as I know, nothing has changed. That's why we're here, right? So he can get one step closer to leaving."

"Aw, hon," Hannah said, slinging an arm around her. "Just have faith. If you two are supposed to work out, you will find a way."

Abby didn't want to think about it, really, and she also didn't want to rain on Hannah's fun, so she just smiled and nodded.

Right now, she was just focusing on the moment.

Hannah grinned, nudging her in the side as she ogled the guys' backsides. "They sure are a couple of hotties, though, huh?"

Abby had to grin, taking a long peek at how well Reece wore his jeans as they approached the SUV.

"You said it," she agreed, and they laughed the rest of the way to the car, the guys watching them curiously as they opened doors, climbed in and headed to the track.

THE CONDO WAS SPACIOUS and modern, with a huge picture window that looked out over the racetrack. Abby was thrilled that she had come along on the trip, not only to be with Reece and Hannah, but also because she had never been to a track except for Watkins Glen, which was a great racetrack, but with it being almost in her backyard didn't have the same kind of excitement.

Like some people enjoyed the beauty of baseball parks or tennis greens, she felt a zing of excitement run down her spine as she scrutinized the raceway. The track wasn't completely empty, though the stands were, but workers were getting ready for preseason events, and she'd seen one driver out on a test drive earlier that morning.

She couldn't help but shiver, watching. She enjoyed the thrill of the speed and the noise, but it had all been so distant before. Now it was real, and it would be Reece in that car, speeding around the curves.

"You're like a kid in a candy shop," Reece said, smiling as he slipped his hands over her shoulders, enjoying her excitement at being involved in his world. This wasn't Formula One, but people who were in racing and who really enjoyed the sport had to respect both circuits, regardless of the debates that always raged among fans about which was superior.

"It's pretty amazing," she said, snuggling back against him. "I'm glad I came."

"Me, too," he murmured.

The night before, they'd gone for a late dinner with Hannah and Brody and then out to walk around the town, as neither Hannah nor Abby had ever been to the area.

It was quite an experience, as they ate in a restaurant that had Brody's picture on the wall, and as they were interrupted by fans of both drivers for pictures and autographs. Both men were gracious and friendly, and Abby had watched in wonder, seeing a whole new side to Reece. He was a well-known public figure. She knew that, but it had never really hit her until now how famous he actually was in this world. And he was here, with her.

It was hard for her to get her mind around it, but she was learning not to second-guess everything.

Brody's condo was huge and, luckily, provided three large, separate sleeping quarters, which Brody often lent to visiting friends and family, or his team. It was immaculate, but not homey, obviously more of a practical investment for Brody than a place he had any emotional attachment to.

"Shouldn't you be at the track with Brody?" she asked, not wanting him to leave, but also wanting to support him, not become a distraction.

Reece seemed to have other ideas, sliding his hands over her hips and up her stomach to cover her breasts, and she couldn't deny the wave of lust that shook her to her toes as they stood before the large window.

They weren't very likely being watched by anyone. The scattering of people who were on the track were busy with their own concerns. Still, the idea of being here, so visible, turned her on.

"You have to drive today," she said on a groan as he nibbled her earlobe.

"I know, and I'm kind of on edge. I need to relax, burn off some energy. You have any ideas?"

She had nothing but ideas.

"What about our game?"

"We can just let off steam, maybe," he said, nipping at her neck and easing her shirt up, sliding his hands beneath as he pressed his hardness against her bottom.

"Oh, okay, then," she said, happy to pursue the satisfaction that had been keeping her in a constant state of wanting. The night before, she had done to him as he had to her, kissing him everywhere, taking him into her mouth and bringing him to the edge, but not finishing. They'd come back down to earth with kisses, eventually falling into an exhausted sleep.

In a strange way, she liked it. What had been frustration turned to something else, a kind of constant promise of intimacy that she had never imagined.

She turned in his arms, pulling his head down for a kiss, after he got rid of her shirt and undid her bra. "One of us has too many clothes on," she said, reaching for the buckle of his belt and undoing it.

Things were getting hot quickly, and she didn't recognize the sound filling the room, but then realized it was her phone.

"Let it go to message," Reece said, drawing on her breast so sweetly she gasped.

"I can't," she said breathlessly, pulling away gently. "I'll see what's up and be right back," she promised.

When she grabbed her phone, she saw it was her insurance agent. She answered immediately.

"Ms. Harper?"

"Yes?" Her heart was in her throat and she couldn't say more.

"Good news. The second fire inspector deemed the fire accidental. We can continue with paying the claim, as planned."

Relief made her hands tremble, and she felt tears sting her eyes. "Oh, thank you so much. Really, I appreciate you doing this so quickly," she said, her voice thick.

"You're very welcome—we do try to do the best for our clients, and a call from your father's friend helped me speed things along," he said with a smile. "Merry Christmas, Miss Harper. We'll be in touch."

She put the phone down and tried to compose herself before she turned back to Reece, but he was already there, turning her to him, taking in her tears. "What is it? What happened?"

She bit her lip and told him everything. He looked surprised, concerned and confused.

"Abby, why didn't you talk to me about this? It has to have been worrying you sick," he said, pulling her in next to him, his chin resting on her head as he rubbed her shoulders.

"I just never could. The timing was always wrong. I worried, at the start, that you might go ahead and sell to Keller if you thought that I wouldn't be financially viable, and then we had our blowup, and now we're just back together, and it's all been crazy," she said, hoping he understood.

He tipped her face up to meet his gaze.

"I guess I can understand why you'd think that, before,

but I hope you trust me with more than your body by now. I wouldn't do anything to hurt you, Abby, ever."

"I know. It's just been…intense. But when they pay out, I might be able to use the funds as a down payment on your property. It'll take everything I have, but if you're willing to work with me, I could do it," she said, holding her breath again.

He nodded, though there was a strange glint in his eye that she couldn't quite read. "I'd like nothing better than for you to have that land. I'll do whatever it takes to sell Winston Vineyards to you," he said. "But what about your own property?"

"At some point I'll repair our house, go back to living there. It's my home, but I won't build new tasting rooms. Yours are so much larger and nicer. If it's okay with you, I thought I might change your house into a bed-and-breakfast," she said, gauging his reaction. "That way it maintains the house, and puts it to good use."

He nodded. "That's smart."

"I'm glad you approve," she said with a smile, feeling lighter by the second. "I would keep your family's vines, too, though I would probably slowly transition the entire operation over to organic."

"Mom and Dad will love hearing that," he said.

The lightness of having things worked out made her dizzy. Reece was going to sell to her. It was going to be okay.

It would be financially tight for many years, but she'd be able to keep her legacy—and his—in place. That was worth everything.

"So, where were we?" she said, sliding her hands up under his shirt, and watching his eyes darken with desire. "I think we were loosening you up for your drive this afternoon?"

He groaned, looking at the clock. "I really do have to meet Brody. I suppose we'll have to…wait."

She smiled, kissing him again. "That's okay. It can be our celebration after you finish your drive."

Her heartbeat raced as she said the words, determined to be supportive and appreciate what they had, for now. The good news from the agent didn't reduce her anxiety about Reece driving, or about him eventually leaving. After all, that was why he was here—to get a second chance at his old life, even if she couldn't be part of it. She was with him now, so she shut out the rest and focused on that as he erased her thoughts with one more scorching kiss before he left.

REECE RAN HIS HAND OVER the hood of the car—it was a beauty, and he was anxious to get out on the track, his nerves banished. He felt great.

The stock car was heavier and built out far differently than those he drove for Formula One, not as low or aerodynamic, but it was a powerful beast, and it would put him to the test.

He knew he could do this. He was ready.

"Feeling good?" Brody asked, walking up beside him, handing him a helmet.

"Yeah. Yeah, I am."

"Let's go then," his buddy said with a slap on his shoulder. "They have everything set up and won't time the first run, so you can get a feel for it, but we'll time a second and third."

He tried to pretend this was as informal as Brody

said, but Reece knew a couple of reporters had caught wind of this drive, and asked to come on site. He'd allowed it. It was risky, but he had nothing to lose at this point.

"Sounds good," Reece said, pulling the helmet on, adjusting and testing the microphone as he prepared to slide himself into the tight spot, the men suddenly gathered around him ready to strap him to the seat.

Before he did so, however, he glanced up and saw Abby, waiting just beyond the perimeter with Hannah and a few other onlookers.

He waved, and she blew him a kiss back.

"You ready, Romeo?" Brody teased and Reece slid into the seat and got prepped.

Minutes later, all systems checked and ready, it was up to him now. Reece had driven this track once or twice before, never officially, but as he looked ahead, everything fell into place.

The world outside of the car dropped away as he pulled forward and got a feel for the smooth, powerful growl of the engine. Something very close to arousal flowed through him, and he became completely focused as he started a first lap, taking it slow at first, getting into the groove.

"God, this feels good," he said with gusto into the mic.

"You're looking good," he heard Brody respond with a knowing laugh.

Closing one lap, Reece got serious and picked up speed, moving the tach up to about 7000 rpms. He took the next corner perfectly, smiling.

This was right. This was where he belonged.

He did a few more laps and pulled in, signaling that he was ready for a timed run.

A short while later, he was off again, punching up the speed, testing the car, his reflexes and his body.

All seemed in working order, and he pulled in a few seconds later, listening over the radio for his time.

"I can do better," he said, to himself as much as to the guys on the other side.

This time, he went for it, watching the yellow light come on that told him he was pushing into the higher area of speeds that could disqualify a driver from a win, but he wasn't competing with anyone but himself and the clock.

He pushed it a little more, coming into the last lap, and caught his breath, cursing as a sharp pain shot up his calf to his knee, causing him to lose focus slightly, and the car wavered on the track.

Cold sweat broke out as he controlled the car, fishtailing slightly, trying to ignore the pain.

"Again," he ground out over the mic, even though Brody was saying no.

"One more."

He managed one more set of laps, clocking a decent time, though slower than he'd have liked.

But he had to stop, he knew, because the pins and needles were so intense, he couldn't feel the accelerator with his foot.

The frustration was more painful, but he swallowed it as he unbuckled himself and was pulled out. When he was set on his feet, his left leg faltered slightly, and he caught it in time to save himself public humiliation.

Brody noticed, and did him the favor of distracting those who were watching.

Abby noticed, too. She was as white as a sheet, staring at him with dark eyes.

A second later, she launched herself at him, and if not for the car behind him they would have both gone down.

"You were wonderful," she said, but she was trembling from head to toe.

"Hey, what's wrong?" he asked. "You're crying."

"I'm so happy for you, and that you are here again. I thought you were going to crash when you fishtailed—it scared me," she said. "But you didn't. You did it," she said, hugging him tightly again.

"My leg went buzzy on me," he said, disgusted with himself, adrenaline still surging through him, his own hands shaking. "I needed to do better."

He figured this was it. He'd made the drive, but his warble was going to be the thing everyone focused on. The thing that would convince the sponsors not to take a chance on him.

"It was respectable, considering," Brody interrupted. "What happened?"

"Lost feeling in my leg—or rather, pins and needles were too intense for me to apply as much pressure as I should. I lost focus for a moment," Reece admitted.

"You controlled it, and your time was decent. Still, your cars and tracks are a lot different, more unpredictable," Brody said, sliding one arm around Hannah and the other rubbing the back of his neck in an obviously nervous gesture. "Maybe if you rest one more season and let your body heal, you'll be in better shape next—"

"I can't do that, Brody, and you know it," Reece said. His leg was a little better now that he was out of his cramped position, but it still bothered him. "This will either convince them or not," he said, thanking his friend and shaking his hand. The chance to prove himself was was all he could ask for, but even Reece knew the drive hadn't gone as well as he needed it to. Not well enough for sponsors to risk millions of dollars on him.

Still, he had done it, and he was going to celebrate, like he had promised Abby.

"Hannah and I have plans tonight—you two are okay on your own?" Brody asked as they left the track.

"Yeah, we'll be fine. You guys have fun—we fly out early?"

"Yeah, see you in the morning."

They parted ways out in the lot after Reece had changed and met Abby where she waited for him outside.

"So, you want to go out and celebrate that I didn't completely wipe out?" he said with humor he wasn't completely feeling.

She touched his face, her eyes fierce. "You did better than that—you had one lapse, and I've seen drivers do a lot worse. We should celebrate because you did *well*."

Reece pulled her in, hugging her tight to his chest, a feeling of warmth and a tangle of other emotions washing over him. To keep himself from thinking about it, he found her mouth, nibbled at it, then kissed her more deeply, soaking up her warmth and her taste and everything that was Abby.

He wanted to hold on to her forever. He loved her, he thought, gazing beyond the open track. The realization didn't come as a surprise, more of a relief. He'd been struggling with his emotions for days, and it felt good to just set them free. He didn't know if he had room for both loves in his life, but he wanted to try.

12

BACK AT THE ROOM, Abby was relieved that her stomach had settled and her hands had finally stopped shaking. She hadn't realized how afraid she'd been for Reece until he actually started to drive.

As she watched the bright blue car covered with logos make laps, she'd relaxed and cheered him on, and when he'd lost control for that handful of seconds, her heart thudded in her chest, and she'd found herself propped up by Hannah.

All she could think of was him dying in that car, and it had flattened her.

The thought of life without him was suddenly impossible.

She loved him. It was a mistake, but she knew it clear down to her bones in the second that the car had fishtailed, and she knew she couldn't stand the idea of losing him, or of him being hurt again.

Lost in her thoughts as they entered the condo, she wandered into the bedroom with the idea of freshening up and maybe taking a nap, and saw several large boxes, all wrapped in bright Christmas wrapping, waiting on the bed.

"What's all this?" she asked Reece, who stood just behind her.

"For you. Open them. This one first," he said, handing her a large, flat box.

"But…it's not even Christmas yet, and I didn't buy anything for you," she objected.

"Just open it, Abby," he said, giving her a patient look.

She did, and set the box down, pulling out the most lovely emerald-green silk dress she had ever seen. A modest scooped bodice was held by lacy spaghetti straps, nipping in at the waist and flaring out around the knee in an ultrafeminine way.

"Reece, it's gorgeous," she breathed, and she sucked her breath back in, coughing as she saw the name of the designer. "Oh, no…this is too much."

"It's what I wanted to buy you. I saw it when we were out yesterday, and I knew it would be perfect on you. And it's warm enough to wear it down here," he said.

"Now?"

"We're going out tonight," he said. "On a date. We haven't had time for that. We need to make time."

"Oh. Reece, I'm so—I'm so…" She tried to find words, but she put the dress down and didn't know what to say. She didn't know what this meant, and she hated the confused rush of thoughts, hopes and doubts that crowded her mind.

"Open the others," he said, pushing her back to the pile of boxes.

"It's too much. The dress is enough."

"What, are you wearing it barefoot or with your boots?" he teased.

She noticed the size of one of the boxes was perfect for shoes, and leapt on it. She couldn't resist shoes, and he was right, she had to have something for the dress.

When she pulled out the sexy, strappy black stilettos, she groaned. "I think I am in lust," she said, petting the soft leather.

"I can't wait to see them on you." He handed her another smaller box, grinning devlishly.

Seeing that he was enjoying her opening the gifts as much as she was enjoying receiving them, she unwrapped the next one, and paused. The box itself was made from black leather with the word *Naughty* embossed on the top.

Taking the lid off, she saw a pair of shiny new handcuffs.

Her heart began to race.

"I want you to wear those tonight, too," he said. "Later," he corrected, his eyes burning hot.

She looked up at him. "I can do that."

The last box, also black leather, said *Nice* on the top.

She smiled. "How can nice be as fun as naughty?"

"Open it and see."

She did, and saw a small bottle of cinnamon massage oil—edible—and she smiled. She lifted it, opening the bottle, the spicy scent greeting her, and she put a dab on her finger, then tasted it, meeting Reece's eyes.

"That is nice," she said, drawing her finger out from between her lips in a sexy gesture, watching his jaw become tense with desire.

But there was one more thing in the box, and she pulled out a small black satin bag, from which a sparkling silver chain fell out into her palm. She lifted it with shaking fingers, a flawless emerald teardrop winking at her in the low light of the room.

"It's beautiful, but I can't possibly accept this, Reece," she said, looking up at him.

He pulled her to her feet, and into his arms for a tight hug followed by a deep kiss.

"Please, I want you to. I want to see you in that dress and the necklace, and then we're coming back here, and it will be my turn to unwrap you," he said, trailing his tongue down her neck, making her shiver.

REECE KNEW HE WAS PLAYING with fire. It'd be hours before he could go back to the room and enjoy Abby's body in every way he imagined.

They sat at a private table at the back of one of his favorite restaurants, the lush bougainvillea and palms surrounding them, a half-finished bottle of wine on the table between them.

Abby was beyond gorgeous in the dress he'd picked out for her when he had snuck out earlier in the day, his plan in place. Hannah had been his coconspirator, and he felt a serious wave of pride and possession as he and Abby had entered the restaurant. He knew every man there envied him, and rightfully so.

Her eyes were as bright as the emerald that lay against her skin, and he got hard every time he thought about their using his other gifts.

"Would you like to dance?" he asked, as the band started to play a slow romantic tune.

She smiled, her eyes soft with the effects of wine and their relaxing time together.

Though she kept silent, he stood. "Dance with me, Abby," he said, his heart hammering in his chest. He wanted to give her everything, which was the source of his dilemma.

She put her hand in his, and it was like a fantasy as they walked onto the dance floor. Amid other couples who swayed together under the Christmas lights hung round the room, they danced to a sexy jazz version of "Have Yourself A Merry Little Christmas."

He pulled her close, pressing his lower body against her and letting her feel how aroused he was. He smiled into her neck as he felt her fingers curl into his jacket.

The dress was a mere scrap between them—another reason he'd picked it out, and he felt her nipples bead under the thin fabric. He moved to the music, letting his chest brush against them, and felt her shudder.

"Reece," she breathed, burying her face against his chest, sounding like she was barely holding on.

It was the sexiest moment of his life. They were in the middle of a crowd of people, and he discreetly leaned in to kiss the curve of her neck, while letting his hand brush her pebbled nipple. She came apart in his arms as they danced.

He captured her surprised gasp with a kiss, the shock of sensation moving through her as she moaned into his mouth, the music offering some disguise. He nearly lost control himself, but somehow managed to hold on.

Later, he thought, smiling at the idea of peeling this dress away, using the handcuffs and the oil. However, he wanted her to leave the necklace and stilettos on.

"Reece, that was…" She paused, looking up at him with smoky eyes and flushed cheeks.

"I know," he murmured, dipping to catch her mouth in another kiss, and keeping her in his arms for several more turns around the dance floor.

He really didn't want this to end—ever—and that was where the danger lay.

The day had been one he wouldn't soon forget—the drive, even though he had had a lapse, was more or less successful, but it was Abby's support that made it shine for him. She made him feel like he could do anything.

She knew he had to leave, that he would go back to racing, and yet she gave herself to him completely, and supported him completely, as well.

He loved her, and he wanted it all—he wanted to race, and he wanted Abby, for good.

He barely noticed the music had stopped, until light applause from the group shook him out of his deep thoughts.

"This has been wonderful," Abby said, looking up at him. "But can we go back to the condo now? Please?"

Her sexy plea shook him with desire, and he nodded, retrieving her shawl and paying the bill. She was the only Christmas gift he ever wanted.

REECE SET FORTH, paying great attention to every aspect of Abby's body. He loved how he could find some new spot that would make her whimper or gasp and when she insistently wove her fingers into his hair, directing him as to what she needed.

She was beautiful but real, smart but modest, sexier

than hell and everything he could ever imagine wanting in a woman.

Limp from his intimate kissing, he carried her to the bed. Slowly he took the sexy shoes off, kissing her ankles and massaging her feet, still sifting through his emotions as he stood to take his own clothes off and join her on the bed.

"No talking," she said, putting a finger against his lips. "Just make love to me, okay?" He was glad to oblige, covering her completely as he drove deep inside. Bodies moving in harmony, their patience and seduction paid off in a series of powerful orgasms that left them both breathless and hanging on to each other.

"I love you, Abby," he said, feeling the truth of what he told her as much as anything he had ever known in his life.

She studied him, as if wondering if she had heard correctly.

"Reece," she said, sighing. "I love you, too."

He had not realized how he'd been holding his breath.

Joy coursed through him. "I've loved you forever, Abby, it just took me a long time to realize it," he said, leaning in to kiss her softly, tenderly, trying to communicate everything he was feeling. It seemed impossible. "Come back with me. To France. Please."

His question hung in the dark between them, and he knew her answer before she even said it.

"I can't…you know that. I mean, I could visit, I could come to see you, but I can't leave the vineyards."

Everything inside of him sank. "You can. We can make it work."

They parted, and pushed back on the pillows, facing each other. He had to convince her, somehow.

"Reece, you know how you said racing was your passion, the thing you loved?"

"Mmm-hmm."

She shrugged her shoulder slightly. "That's what the vineyards are for me. I love it there. It's my home, but it's also my passion, and it feels important to preserve that legacy. My parents left me the business they spent their lives building. I can't just abandon that."

"We could work it out. You could get a manager, and we could come back as often as we needed to—" he said, but she interrupted.

"And what would I do in Europe? Follow you around to the races? As much as I want to be with you, that's not a life I want. And…I don't know if I could do it. It was hard, watching you drive today. I was proud of you, happy for you, but I don't think I could stand there and watch if something bad happened again. I just… couldn't."

He pulled her in, not wanting her to see how disappointed he was, though he knew she was right. He shouldn't ask her to make this sacrifice for him.

"It's selfish of me to want you to come with me, you're right, and I suppose it's time I face facts. They aren't going to take me back," he said, weaving his fingers through hers and not wanting to let go. "Maybe Brody is right, maybe another year, or maybe not. Maybe it's time for me to move on to other things."

"Do you mean…are you saying…?"

"I'll stay. I want to be with you, Abby, and I think today proved that it's the right choice for me to make."

She was quiet in his arms, and he wanted to see her face.

"You okay? I thought you would be happier."

"I am," she said, looking at him closely. "I just don't want you giving up on your dreams for me."

"Maybe it's just time I learn to chase a new dream, don't you think? One you and I could share together?"

She smiled then, and reached up to kiss him.

Reece let the passion rise again, losing himself in Abby, and setting his doubts aside. He loved her. He was making the right decision. He had to be.

13

ABBY PANICKED WHEN she walked out of Reece's kitchen, the scent of fire meeting her nose. Following it, she found Reece down behind the lower barn on his property, a fire burning in an area he cleared, and some contraption built above that held a wine barrel in place.

"I wondered what you were up to," Abby said. He'd spent most of his time here since they had gotten back from Daytona the day before. She'd been constantly busy, too busy to investigate before now.

"It's a wine barrel," Reece said, grinning.

"I see that. I knew your Dad was a cooper, but I didn't know you were."

"I'm not," Reece clarified, rubbing his hands together and leaning in for a kiss before he nodded to her to follow him into the barn. "Dad always tried to get me into it, but I was never interested. I forgot he had this workshop. I figured I'd see what I could remember, and looked up the rest on the Internet." He checked the steaming barrel suspended above the fire. "That's my first one. We'll see what happens."

"Wow, I am impressed. You are a man of many talents," she said, reaching up to kiss him again and loving the smoky, earthy scents that surrounded them.

Still, something was off, and she'd felt it in the four days since they had returned. Since he had told her he was staying, she knew. It was what she wanted. She loved him, and she wanted him here, but some undefinable layer of tension seemed to run underneath them now, and while she thought it was good for Reece to get back in touch with his family's history and pursuits, he himself had said this was never his passion.

Driving was his passion, and he was giving it up, for her.

So she had made a few calls herself, namely, one to Joe, the man Reece had been talking with before. His number was left on Reece's phone, and Abby called, and talked to him, to find out if Reece really was out of the sport.

As it turned out, just the opposite.

News of Reece's test run had spread and, true to form, fans were cheering him on, wanting him back. Joe knew it, and sponsors knew it, and they were willing to give him some test runs in Europe, to see how things went.

They wanted him there soon, and they had been going to call him, when Abby had taken the tiger by the tail and contacted them.

Her chest tightened as she pulled back from Reece's increasingly passionate kiss.

"I have something to tell you," she said, trying to sound normal, but her heart hurt a little, even though she knew this was the right thing to do. She loved him, and that meant not having him just walk away from his dream for her.

"Yeah, can it wait?" Reece said teasingly, dipping in for another kiss.

She laughed, evading him, and putting a hand on either shoulder, she made him listen as she told him about her phone call to Joe.

Everything from confusion to disbelief to excitement passed across his face, and finally, he shook his head and pulled her in closer.

"I can't believe you did that," he said huskily against her hair.

"I didn't do anything. They were going to call you anyway. And you know you have to go. Reece, you have to."

He didn't say anything, but she'd seen the light, the hope, in his face. She wouldn't let him stay here and give it all up.

"So what do we do, then? I don't want to lose you," he said, the emotion in his voice sincere.

"I guess we'll just have to see what happens. Maybe we can visit each other, definitely we'll talk on the phone," she said. She feared her tone betrayed her, that maintaining a relationship that way probably wasn't realistic. "It'll only be for another few years, and then we could make some decisions about being together for good, right?"

REECE HELD HER TIGHT, his mind spinning with the news. They wanted him back! But he also wanted to be with Abby. Conflicted, he didn't know how to answer her question.

He was on the circuit for months at a time. Some of the guys' families did stay home, especially when there were kids and other considerations. Not all of the wives traveled with their husbands, but a few did.

Still, those couples had the deeper connection of years together, a marriage to return to. He didn't know if what he had with Abby was too new, too tenuous to endure that kind of separation. The realization hit him like a ton of bricks, and he lifted her face up to his, kissing her.

"Aw, Abby, don't cry."

"I can't help it. I love you, and you love me, but I can't see how we can make this work," she said, her voice tight and pained. "I want to, but…"

He held her tight, unable to stand that she was suffering, even a little, because of him.

He knew how to make it right. They could make it work—and they would. He was going back to Europe, and he had no idea what the future held, but he knew two things for sure: he had to at least try to get back to racing, and he couldn't lose Abby.

The answer to both seemed clear.

"Abby?" he asked, his heart thundering.

"Yeah?"

"Will you marry me?"

ABBY WAS UP TO HER EARS in satin, flowers and bridesmaids.

Two days before Christmas, the winery was decorated, and everything was ready for the wedding reception. She'd been working overtime—an understatement—to make sure it was all perfect.

Looking around at the young women in beautiful,

deep red satin Christmas gowns, it put to rest the notion that bridesmaids wore ugly dresses. These were chic and stylish, and Abby thought of the beautiful silk dress Reece had given her. It was far too light to wear, even indoors, in this climate, but she felt very proper back in her basic black business dress.

She lifted her hand to the emerald that lay against her throat. She hadn't taken it off since Reece had put it on for her that night in Florida.

The winery looked magical. Christmas lights were strung everywhere along the reception-room ceiling and through the entryway. He'd helped her string them before he left. It had only been four days and it felt like so much longer.

A fire crackled in the fireplace. The tables were set with fine white china, the glasses were sparkling crystal and Christmas bouquets of holly, poinsettias and white roses decorated each table.

The small band the bride and groom had hired was setting up in the reception room. Specialty bottles of different varieties of both Winston and Maple Hills wines, uniquely labeled for the bridal couple's special day, looked elegant on the tables, ready for each guest to take one home.

All they needed now was the bride and groom, who were taking a little longer arriving, so the bridesmaids and some of the groomsmen—also handsome in gray tuxedos with deep red cumberbuns—milled around, tasting appetizers and enjoying some drinks.

Abby felt incredibly alone even though she was in a roomful of people. Her throat tightened with emotions she had been fighting off since Reece had left for France.

He'd had to go. She wanted him to go. His sponsors were asking him to come back. No promises, but they were giving him a chance. It was exactly as Reece had predicted—everyone loved a comeback.

She wasn't about to stand in his way, and she made that clear by refusing his proposal. It had been the hardest thing she'd ever done. He wasn't angry, but he also told her he intended to keep on asking.

She figured he would, maybe, for a while. Then his life would take over, and he would know they'd made the right decision. Maybe, in a few years, things would be different, she thought, but found it hard to believe. So many things could happen in that time.

On top of that, Hannah was gone, too, staying in Florida with Brody. She had offered to come back, but Abby had released her from that responsibility. Abby was glad to take it on by herself, to have so much work to do that maybe she wouldn't think too much.

That would come to an end after the wedding, when she would close down through New Year's.

And do what? With whom?

Well, she thought, she had Beau and Buttercup.

She couldn't even move forward on plans for the reconstruction, since the city more or less closed down between Christmas and New Year's.

Reece had asked her to come to France for Christmas and stay the week. She was tempted. She'd never seen France, but would it just be extending the torture for both of them?

She didn't know if she'd be able to leave if she went there to be with him.

The fact was, though they loved each other, they had both chosen their individual passions over being together. Who was going to budge? Who should give up what they loved? What kind of foundation was that for a marriage? And how could they even think of getting married when they had only been lovers for less than a month? It was so unfair. It went against every grain of common sense she had, and at the same time, she knew he was the only one for her.

She was shaken from her reverie as applause scattered around her, growing louder with hoots and whistles as the bridal couple arrived, and Abby joined in. Sandra looked absolutely gorgeous, and as the party started, she took her place with the caterers and other party organizers, making sure all went well.

Seeing Sandra and her new husband so happy filled Abby with doubt—had she made the wrong choice?

Was being here more important than being with Reece, and supporting him as he made his way back onto the circuit? He would only be racing for another few years at most, and then they could open their own winery, wherever they wanted. Everyone else in her life was gone, out living their lives, but this was her life, her dream—wasn't it?

She didn't know anymore. What was the right thing to do? She had so many plans to revive this place, and at the very least, she needed to be here during the rebuilding to see that through.

Her heart was heavy, and she was exhausted as the hours wore on. Late in the evening, the caterers gone, the party was still lasting long past her ability to stay. She needed to be alone, to go off and lick her wounds in private.

As she started back toward the house, she saw headlights turn into the drive. It was very late for anyone to be arriving—a late wedding guest maybe?

The car came closer, and her heart leapt as she recognized the driver. She ran toward the car as the door opened, feeling happy for the first time in days.

"Oh, Mom, Dad! I'm so happy you're here!"

Her parents had no idea what to do when she launched herself at them and broke down in tears.

THEY WANTED HIM BACK.

While the younger guy who had been in line to replace him had been close to doing just that, the media coverage of Reece's trial in Florida, coupled with an interview that hit the French and U.S. papers, had fans insisting they wanted Reece back on the track. The response was overwhelming, especially online, and Reece had as hard a time believing it as anyone.

He should have been thrilled.

Snow was falling in Paris as he sat in a conference room with his manager, the car's owner, the sponsor reps and God knew who else. They had been talking incessantly about new acupuncture methods, hiring him a personal physical therapist and doing whatever was necessary to get him back in a car, winning races.

It was what he wanted, so why was he sitting here thinking about what Abby was doing? Today was the wedding, and she was probably so busy she hadn't even thought of him. He'd sent her an e-mail, left her a phone message earlier, but hadn't heard back.

He still couldn't believe she had made that call—she hadn't set any of this in motion, of course, but the fact that she had been willing to let him go, to put his dreams first, still stunned him. If it was possible, he loved her more every time he thought about her.

He didn't know how he was going to manage it, but he wasn't going to lose her. She'd said no this time, and that was fine. She was right, again. It was too soon, maybe he had proposed for the wrong reasons. He had been desperately trying to find a way to make it all work, but he knew he really did want her, and only her, in his life. Maybe she'd say yes the next time, or the time after that.

He didn't plan on giving up.

"Reece? Can you be in Italy in two days? You can start training now. We want you back in shape and ready to go as soon as possible," his manager said. Tony was a good guy, but Reece swore he saw dollar signs flashing in his eyes for a moment.

Reece wasn't a person—an actual human being—to anyone gathered in this room. He was a commodity, a product.

He listened as they discussed liability issues, if the car would be covered, how much they stood to lose if he crashed again, what the risks were with insurance if anyone thought he wasn't up to racing in the first place.

He was. Even with his problems at Daytona, he knew he could do it. No more cold hands or nerves at the thought of getting behind the wheel, but what if the worst happened?

He could care less about the car, or anything else. His doubts weren't borne of fear of dying, but of fear of never seeing Abby again. Could he live with that?

No.

"Reece?" Tony asked again, sounding irritated. "I hope your focus is better when you get back in a car," he said.

Some muffled laughter and commentary met the remark, and Reece smiled. He couldn't believe what he was about to do.

"Two days from now? That's Christmas day," he said, sparking off a round of confused glances around the conference table.

"So what? You need to be on this ASAP and 24/7 if it's going to work. The docs will clear you, but only if you sign a contract and follow the physical regimen to the letter."

Reece looked out the window at the snow, thinking, of all things, about Abby's pork roast. That was certainly not going to be part of his training. He'd invited her to come see him next week—but now he would be in training, out of touch twelve to eighteen hours a day, every day.

He wouldn't ask her to do that. No way would he say she had to come all the way over here and then form her life around his crazy racing schedule, content to see him in whatever cracks of time he had left.

It was why he'd never gotten into relationships in the first place.

"Reece, what the—"

"I'm sorry, Tony, I can't do it this week. I have other plans for Christmas," he said, amazed at how easy it was. Abby had given him the gift of going after his dreams, after what he really wanted, and that was what he was going to do.

"You...you *what?*"

"Listen, I appreciate this. I thought it was what I wanted, but I need to be home for Christmas."

"Home? Reece, you are home. This is home."

He grinned again, feeling incredibly giddy as he torpedoed his racing career for good.

"No, home is where Abby is."

"WHY DID YOU DECIDE to come back?" Abby asked, wrapped up in a blanket that smelled like Reece, having a very late-night cup of hot chocolate with her parents.

Her mom and dad shared a somewhat guilty look, and Abby peered at them over her mug. "Tell me."

"Well, to be completely honest," her mother began, "Hannah called us."

Abby groaned. "I'm sorry, she shouldn't have done that. I'm fine."

Her mom looked at her, and Abby felt like she was ten again.

"She told us Reece proposed."

Abby groaned a second time, closing her eyes and planning what she would do to her friend the next time she saw her. It wouldn't be pretty.

"We had no idea you and Reece were an item, let alone so serious," her dad said.

"We...it's complicated. He has his life, I have mine. The two don't match up so well."

"Why is that?"

"He has to be in Europe, racing, hopefully, and I have to be here, rebuilding and running the vineyards."

"Is that really what you want, honey?" her mom asked, as if seeing right through her. "It's clear just by the look on your face, and how you cried your heart out a little while ago, that you love him. So why aren't you in France with an engagement ring on your finger for Christmas?"

Abby opened her mouth, gaped, started to say something. "Mom," she began, "I love it here, and I have responsibilities, and—"

"They sound more like excuses than reasons, Abigail," her father said.

"Wait," she said, putting her hand up. "You know how much work this is, and it's even more so now with the fire and the reorganizing. I have to be here…right? And besides…" she said, but didn't finish her thought.

"Besides, what?"

"I don't know. There was this moment, when Reece lost control of the car for a minute, down in Daytona."

"We saw it on the news. He pulled it back."

"I know. But it scared me to death. What if he hadn't? What if he died, right there in front of me? I don't know if I can handle that."

"Would you rather it happens when you're not there? When you're not the last person he sees before he races? The person he woke up with that morning? I'm sorry to be harsh, honey, but your father and I have seen a lot of pain and suffering in the last few months, and one thing I can tell you is that you can't avoid it. If Reece crashed, would your pain be any less for staying here?

Would it be better not to have married him and had that time together?"

Abby gaped, wordless in response to her parents' questions. That Reece could crash, could get hurt or worse, knowing that she hadn't wanted to be with him, had said no to marrying him. Had let him go...

And what about when he won? When he wanted to celebrate and enjoy life? Didn't she want to share that with him, too? The good and the bad?

"Oh, Mom," she said, a fresh batch of new tears at the realization flooding her eyes.

"It's hard to figure out on your own sometimes, I know," her mom said.

"But if I go...what about here? What about the wineries, and the rebuilding?"

"Well, that was kind of the miracle of Hannah's call. She gave us an excuse to come back."

"She...what? I thought you loved your travel and your work?"

"Oh, we did. It was wonderful, but it made us also realize how precious home was, and how long we had been away. We wanted to come back, to come back to running the vineyard, but we didn't want you to feel like we were intruding or suggesting you weren't doing just fine. When Hannah called, we knew it was the right time to come back. For us, and for you."

"You want to run the vineyard again?"

"Yes, and we have a bit more money in investments set aside, so we can, we think, with the insurance, probably buy Reece out, instead of you doing that and going broke trying." Her mother shook her head. "Really, Abby, didn't we teach you better about leading a balanced life?"

Abby fought the urge to smile. "Hannah really did tell you everything, huh?"

"Yes."

"Remind me to thank her."

Her parents' grins broke out wide, and so did hers. "We'll do that. But you have to get ready."

"Ready? For what?"

Her parents chuckled conspiratorially and her father handed her an envelope with a red ribbon on it.

"You have a morning flight to Paris. Our Christmas gift to you. Go pack."

REECE TURNED INTO the driveway of the house and parked at the edge, party-goers apparently still sleeping from the wedding reception. It was Christmas Eve morning; he had made it home, just in time.

He couldn't wait to sneak in and wake Abby up—he fully intended to make love to her until she agreed to wear the ring he had in his pocket. It was his mission, he thought with a smile.

As he climbed the steps to the porch, he paused, looking out over the snowy fields down toward the grapes. All of the trees Abby had put in the yard sparkled and were lit, and Christmas was in the air. He never really understood what people meant when they said that, but he could feel it, right now, and he knew. Some of her Christmas magic must have rubbed off on him, he guessed.

He heard the door open behind him and spun, expecting to see Abby, but found himself facing an older man instead.

"Uh, hi," Reece said, peering at the man more closely. He looked familiar. "I'm Reece, I live—"

"Oh, I know who you are," the man said, letting out a belting laugh. He was then was joined by an older woman, whose eyes went wide.

Reece's did, too. He could see Abby in her mother's face and laughed as well.

"Mr. and Mrs. Harper! What a surprise," he said. It *was* a surprise. His sneaky seduction of Abby would have to wait, he supposed. "It's so nice you made it here for Christmas, and not to be rude, but where is Abby?"

CHRISTMAS AT HANCOCK INTERNATIONAL AIRPORT wasn't exactly what Abby had counted on, but she was going to wait out this flight delay no matter what. It would figure. She had nearly killed herself getting here, unable to fly out of the smaller, Ithaca airport, and now her flight was delayed for weather.

She was going to call Reece and let him know she was coming, but then she thought she would make it a surprise instead—hopefully a happy one. He had invited her, so she hoped he'd be glad to see her.

So, she gave up her seat to a young mother carrying a baby, and paced in front of the gate, willing the delay to be lifted. She couldn't sit still anyway, in spite of getting no sleep, she was wired and eager to get going. The place was crowded, flooded with holiday travelers, and she felt sorry for the mom with the crying baby, and for kids napping against the posts and harried parents.

She paced to the vending machine and looked over the candy selection, and grabbed a chocolate bar, then headed to the Starbucks to get another double-shot expresso.

Her phone rang, and she looked.

Reece.

Her heart trip-hammered in her chest, and her hand shook as she clicked the talk button, though it could have been from the caffeine.

Right.

"Abby, it's Reece," he said.

She laughed. "I know."

"Oh, right. Listen, I just wanted to let you know I've had a change in plans, and I won't be able to meet you in France for the week."

She paused. "What do you mean?"

"Listen, I know you probably weren't planning to come anyway, but I have to be somewhere else, and I didn't want you coming here and ending up finding me gone."

Her heart sank. She looked at the lines of people suddenly in motion as they flooded the gate. The flight was boarding.

Of course it was.

She took a deep breath and got a grip.

"So, where will you be? I'll meet you there. Wherever," she said, determined to make this work.

"Really? You'd meet me anywhere?"

"Yes. Reece, I have a lot to tell you, but things have changed, and…I want to spend Christmas with you, and tell you everything that's happened. I don't care where you are, I just want to be with you."

"I can't wait," he said, but this time the sound of his voice didn't come from the phone, but from right behind her.

She turned, and found herself nose-to-nose with him, and let out a screech that stopped just about everyone around them in their tracks. Throwing herself at him, they nearly both fell over until he got his balance and set her on her feet, saying nothing until he kissed her thoroughly.

"Hi, sweetheart."

"When did you come home? How did you know…?"

He smiled. "I didn't. I was at the house, and your parents said you were taking a flight. I couldn't believe it. I was breaking land-speed records getting here, I think, because I thought I would miss you," he explained.

"You mean…at our house?" she asked, slowly putting two and two together.

"Yeah. I'm back. I didn't want to go through Christmas—or my life—without you."

She was stunned, and lack of breathing threatened to steal words from her, the emotions hitting her too hard, the questions all rising too quickly.

"Breathe, Abby," he said, kissing her again, and making sure she did.

"It was all happening, just as I hoped for," he explained, "but none of it felt right. It wasn't like before. I didn't feel like I was home or happy or doing what I wanted to be doing. I didn't expect it. They were offering me everything I wanted, and all I could think of was that I wanted you. I wanted to be here. I wanted to wake up in bed with you Christmas morning, for the rest of our lives."

Abby almost wondered if she had fallen asleep and was dreaming all of this. She must have said so, because he assured her he was real.

"I love you, Abby," he said, his voice low and full of emotion. "I'm yours, if you want me."

"I love you, too, Reece. And Christmas in bed sounds perfect to me," she whispered, sliding into his arms once and for all.

Epilogue

ABBY BUSTLED AROUND the kitchen, making Reece the most amazing anniversary dinner he could imagine. They ate out at restaurants so often when they were on the road with the new team that she wanted to do something special, and something private. Her parents had gone on a vacation to the house in Talence, leaving Abby and Reece home to watch over the vineyard and enjoy their first anniversary alone together. With that amazing bathroom, she thought with a grin.

She loved the house, and their new life following the races around the U.S. and traveling and working the vineyard in between. Reece and Brody were co-owners of a new racing team now, and they were often surrounded by crowds and people, which was fun and exciting, but Abby wanted her husband to herself tonight. The team was doing very well, and Brody was in charge while Reece took the week off.

It was their first anniversary, after all, and she looked out the kitchen window at the pristine summer countryside. She loved Christmas, but was happy they had waited for a summer wedding. The vineyards were so lovely, and they had been married out among them, over-looking the lake.

She had plans for her husband, who had been teasing her mercilessly for a week, keeping her on edge, dol-ing out his seductions with practiced patience. She was intent on doing whatever was necessary to make him give in to her tonight.

The thought put a sly smile on her face. She didn't think he'd mind. They'd honed the practice of extended sex play and seduction to a fine art.

She checked all of the food, and took another peep at the delectable pastry in the refrigerator that was one of her favorites.

Her plan started now.

Shucking her clothes, she grabbed the sexy apron he'd caught her in that first Christmas and donned only that, taking her coat from the hook and heading down to the workshop Reece had remodeled to continue per-fecting his cooperage. The craft had created a new bond between Reece and his father, as well, which both of them enjoyed, and now many of the barrels in which they aged their wine were made on premises.

She walked into the workshop, which smelled of oak and the delicious scents of wine and burnt wood, and she had come to find the aroma incredibly erotic. Reece was bent over an almost finished cask, cauterizing the opening through which the wine would be poured. She waited for him to finish, enjoying watching him, ap-preciating every sexy muscle in his body as he leaned into his work.

When he finished, he looked up and was unsurprised to find her there.

"Hey," he said, taking off his safety glasses and

crossing to a sink to take off his gloves and wash his hands before he crossed to her, kissing her soundly. "How long have you been there?" he asked.

"Just a minute," she said, love filling her just looking at him. "Dinner is almost done."

"Do we have a few minutes?"

"Sure."

"Isn't it a little hot for a coat?" he said, his eyes drifting down over her bare legs.

She smiled and wiggled her eyebrows. "I didn't think you'd want me walking down from the house in only this," she said as she dropped the coat and watched his eyes darken with lust. "So what did you have in mind?" she asked innocently, raising an eyebrow at some ties attached to a beam that had been put to very good use the evening before.

"I have an anniversary gift for you," he said, his voice a little raspy.

She smiled. "I have one for you, too, back at the house—but it's something we'll want to use there," she said, sending him a sexy look.

"Mmm. Maybe we can come back for yours then," he said, grabbing her by the waist and pulling her up close, where she could feel the extent of his excitement.

"Nope, I'd like mine now, please," she said, poking him in the chest playfully.

"Okay, vixen, come with me," he said, bringing her to a set of newly finished barrels. He opened one bottle and drew two glasses from the tap, a rich Baco that he sniffed, swirled and tasted, then handed hers to her.

"It's perfect, just like you," he said, toying with the apron tie at her neck.

She sipped the rich, fruity wine and groaned in

appreciation as the flavors washed over her. "I don't think I have ever had a wine this complex—how did you get those sorts of sweet, smoky notes in there?"

It was a sexy, sensual wine, and she took another sip, feeling the tie at her neck pull loose.

"I've been experimenting with the barrels. This wine is ours. Like your mom and dad always did, I named it for us, too. Our story," he said. "Happy Anniversary."

"Oh, Reece. This is lovely. What did you name it?"

He put his glass down and pulled her in close as the apron fell away completely.

"Christmas in Bed."

She smiled, so much in love she didn't think she could ever express it, so she just let herself be carried away by his kiss, because Reece was right. It was perfect.

* * * * *

Harlequin Presents® is thrilled
to introduce the first installment of
an epic tale of passion and drama by
USA TODAY *Bestselling Author*
Penny Jordan*!*

When buttoned-up Giselle first meets
the devastatingly handsome Saul Parenti,
the heat between them is explosive....

"LET ME GET THIS STRAIGHT. Are you actually suggesting that I would stoop to that kind of game playing?"

Saul came out from behind his desk and walked toward her. Giselle could smell his hot male scent and it was making her dizzy, igniting a low, dull, pulsing ache that was taking over her whole body.

Giselle defended her suspicions. "You don't want me here."

"No," Saul agreed, "I don't."

And then he did what he had sworn he would not do, cursing himself beneath his breath as he reached for her, pulling her fiercely into his arms and kissing her with all the pent-up fury she had aroused in him from the moment he had first seen her.

Giselle certainly *wanted* to resist him. But the hand she raised to push him away developed a will of its own and was sliding along his bare arm beneath the sleeve of his shirt, and the body that should have been arching away from him was instead melting into him.

Beneath the pressure of his kiss he could feel and taste her gasp of undeniable response to him. He wanted to devour her, take her and drive them both until they were equally satiated—even whilst the anger within him that she should make him feel that way roared and burned its

HPEXP0111

resentment of his need.

She was helpless, Giselle recognized, totally unable to withstand the storm lashing at her, able only to cling to the man who was the cause of it and pray that she would survive.

Somewhere else in the building a door banged. The sound exploded into the sensual tension that had enclosed them, driving them apart. Saul's chest was rising and falling as he fought for control; Giselle's whole body was trembling.

Without a word she turned and ran.

Find out what happens when Saul and Giselle succumb to their irresistible desire in

THE RELUCTANT SURRENDER

Available January 2011 from Harlequin Presents®

HARLEQUIN®

A Romance

FOR EVERY MOOD™

Spotlight on

Classic

Quintessential, modern love stories
that are romance at its finest.

See the next page
to enjoy a sneak peek from
the Harlequin Presents® series.

REQUEST YOUR FREE BOOKS!

2 FREE NOVELS PLUS 2 FREE GIFTS!

HARLEQUIN®

Blaze

Red-hot reads!

COMING NEXT MONTH

Available December 28, 2010

#585 INTO THE NIGHT
Forbidden Fantasies
Kate Hoffmann

#586 THE REBEL
Uniformly Hot!
Rhonda Nelson

#587 IRRESISTIBLE FORTUNE
Wendy Etherington

#588 CAUGHT OFF GUARD
Kira Sinclair

#589 SEALed WITH A KISS
Jill Monroe

#590 JUMP START
Texas Hotzone
Lisa Renee Jones